ACADEMY OBSCURA

THE FLAME WITHIN

CASSIA BRIAR

Wednesday Ink

ACADEMY OBSCURA
Campus Map

A. Dean's Hall
B. Trial Chamber
C. Cortez Dorm
D. Stewart Dorm
E. McIver Dorm
F. Sorrentino Hall
G. Chang Dorm

H. Freeman Dorm
I. Academy Hall
J. Culling House
K. Fotia Hall
L. Nero Hall
M. Gi Hall
N. Aeras Hall

CONTENTS

*To my husband who enthusiastically
reads all my first drafts.*

1

CAPRICE

I was driving fast up the freeway, probably too fast, but it was an evening for speed. The summer between high school and college was supposed to be filled with adventure and recklessness. These were the best days of our lives, after all.

Elena sat in the passenger seat, bright red bikini top showing off her perfect tan. Her long, wavy black hair was twisted into a messy bun.

She cranked up the radio. "Love this song!" Elena started to sing along. She was so tone deaf. I laughed, drumming on the steering wheel.

The last rays of sunlight shone through the driver side window, and I shifted the visor to block it out. My tan arms were showing a faint pinkish hue from the day spent at the beach.

"This summer is the best. And this party is going to be epic," Elena said.

I glanced at her over the top of my sunglasses. We were on our way to crash a University of Maryland Baltimore County party. Both of us would be attending UMBC in the fall. May as well check out their party life now.

I smiled, never sure which one of us was the bad influence over the other. Maybe it didn't matter. Since we met each other sophomore year of high school, we'd been inseparable.

Changing lanes, I zoomed around several cars in a row.

We arrived at the beach, parked, and grabbed our tote bags. Opening the car door, the warm, humid air blasted me, instantly coating my skin with a sheen of sweat.

The sun was setting in the hills behind us. The beach swarmed with college students in shorts and tank tops. At one end was a volleyball net, at the other some tables set up with a row of kegs. In the middle of the sand, the bonfire was about to be lit.

I glanced at Elena. "What you think?"

"Let's start with beer."

We marched over to the kegs and poured ourselves a couple of drinks. I turned around to survey the crowd. Someone had turned up the music and people started to dance in the sand. The hip-hop beat thumped along with my pulse.

"Hey, lovelies." The guy approaching us was buff and tan. His blond hair cut short. He smiled, showing perfect white teeth. Damn, I didn't realize such hotties went to UMBC. He was probably a jerk, most hot guys were.

"Heyyy..." Elena said. She was totally checking him out.

He cozied up to her. "Wanna dance?" He took her hand and led her out to the unofficial dance floor.

I sipped the beer, watching them for a while as the last rays of light disappeared. Chewing on the inside of my cheek, I was unsure of what to do. I could go dance by myself. Or hang out on the side and people-watch.

From across the bonfire, a guy caught my eye. He was wearing sunglasses, which I thought was weird now that the sun had gone down. Even though I couldn't see his eyes, I knew he was looking at me, I could sense it. A shiver ran down my arms.

He moved slowly in my direction. Not directly. He skirted the perimeter of the party, eventually ending up about ten feet from me. He stood in the shadows, just out of reach of the bonfire's light.

I blinked and he vanished. Something about him captured my full attention. More than anything, I wanted to find him, to see him again. I couldn't explain this sudden, overwhelming curiosity.

Intrigued, I approached where I'd last seen him standing. Maybe he'd gone around the side of the restroom building. I circled it. He wasn't anywhere around, yet I thought I could feel his presence. Or at least, it felt like someone was watching me.

Then he appeared behind me. I spun around. He'd taken off the sunglasses. In the dim light, I could make out a defined jawline, broad shoulders, and short dark hair.

He stood so close that I could smell him. A heady scent of fresh spring water and pine.

I swayed toward him. Alarm bells went off in the back of my brain. Something wasn't right about him.

"Look at me." His voice was deep, rich, and compelling.

My eyes lifted to his, which seemed to glow with a faint silver light. I couldn't look away.

"I'm going to kiss you," he said.

I continued to stare up at him, unable to say anything or move. We were in the dark, behind the restrooms where no one could see us.

He grabbed my waist and lifted, stepping forward until I was pinned between him and the concrete wall. All the while, he still held my gaze. His hands slid up from my waist to brush against my breasts, but they didn't linger there. They continued up to palm either side of my face. He licked his lips, then brought his mouth to mine.

His lips were warm and soft, yet demanding. He deepened the kiss. Parting my lips with his tongue.

I felt dizzy, like I'd had too much to drink. But my half consumed beer was still clutched in my hand. It was like this guy had some power over me. Or I was in a dream. None of it seemed real.

The floaty feeling lessened when I noticed his hands had returned to my body. One hand was wrapped around my waist while the other cupped my bikini-encased breast. The warmth of his palm seeped through the thin fabric. He caught my nipple between two fingers. I gasped.

The shock jolted me back to reality. What was I doing? I didn't even know this guy. And I didn't want to be this easy. I'd had sex once. Years ago. My second time was not going to be behind a bathroom with a stranger.

I dropped the beer cup, freeing up my hands to push against his solid chest.

He drew back and locked his gaze on mine. "You will not resist me."

The weird light-headed feeling came back. My body went limp in his arms, and he lowered us to the sun-warmed sand. He leered down at my scantily clad body. That silver glow flaring in his eyes.

When his weight pressed down on me, something snapped alert in my brain again.

I shoved at him with all my strength. He seemed unprepared for it and rolled to the side. I took the opportunity to jump up and run. Twenty feet away, the party was in full swing.

Panicked, I sped through the crowd trying to find Elena. The music was blasting so loud that I couldn't hear anything over it. In the middle, I circled. I didn't see Elena, but the creepy guy was lurking on the outside, his gaze fixed on me. Like a predator waiting for his prey.

Blood rushed in my ears as I spun again, searching for Elena. A million horrible questions popped into my head. How was I going to get out of here? Was the guy Elena danced with a freak too? Had he taken her somewhere?

Then I spotted her. She was with the same blond guy. They were making out by the volleyball net.

I pushed through the twerking bodies to the other side. At a dead run, I closed the distance between me and my friend. Without a word, I grabbed her arm, pulling her toward the car.

"What the hell?" Elena said, struggling to free herself.

"We need to leave. Right now. Questions later." I'd lost my tote, but I didn't care. The car keys were in my shorts pocket. I fished them out. Dropped them on the asphalt. Then picked them up with shaking hands.

"Seriously, what's going on?" Elena wrenched her arm out of my grip.

I faced her. "Get in the car."

Whatever expression I wore must have scared her. Her face paled, and she sprinted around to the passenger side.

I pressed the fob to unlock the car. Just as I reached for the handle, the creep appeared right behind Elena. I screamed.

He spun her around to face him. "Sleep," he commanded.

She fell to the ground. What the hell?

His eyes locked on me. "No human can resist me. Few others can either. What are you?"

I didn't know what he was talking about. His words barely registered. I needed to get Elena and myself out of there. But she lay on the other side of the car at his feet.

The blond that Elena had been making out with approached us. "What's going on here?" he asked.

I stepped closer to him "Help. This creep...he did something to her. He's trying to assault me."

The creep spoke. "She's resisting my compulsion, which is impossible. Be careful. She's not human. I don't know what she is."

Wait. These two knew each other? I moved toward the driver's door.

Blond dude chuckled. "Man, you need to learn the art of subtlety. Now leave them alone." When creep didn't move, Elena's guy said, "Leave. Now." His voice came out strong, almost booming. It was unnatural and freaky as hell.

Creep cursed, but left. The blond strode over to where Elena lay unconscious. He picked her up, opened the car door, and buckled her into the passenger seat. With a glance at me, he said, "Sorry about that. My friend gets a little carried away. "

I didn't care what his excuse was. I started the car, slamming my door shut. As soon as the passenger door closed, I sped out of the parking lot.

I glanced at Elena. She still slept. At least, I hoped she was just sleeping.

My heart was pounding too fast. My hands shook on the steering wheel. That creep had done something to my brain. Like some kind of mind game. Hypnotism, or something. I'd almost given into him. Almost. A chill radiated from my chest. I shivered.

I turned on the radio. The music helped, as I took deep breaths in and out. When I was feeling more stable, I reached over to shake Elena's shoulder. Her eyelids fluttered open. She sat up.

"What's going on?" she asked. "Was I just sleeping?"

I was so relieved she was okay. "Some creep attacked me. Then he went after you, used some kind of hypnotism to make you fall asleep. But that guy you were making out with made the creep go away." That was the best I could sum it up.

"Oh my God, are you all right?" Elena asked, then she cringed. "My head feels foggy."

Frowning, I nodded. "Let's get home."

2

CAPRICE

After dropping off Elena at her parent's house, I drove the block and a half to mine, and parked the old Jetta on the street. There were no sidewalks in our neighborhood, so the lawn came right up to the street.

I sat in the car for a few moments to let my heartbeat settle before facing my foster parents. Trying again to wrap my brain around what had happened tonight, it was no use. Hypnotism? Glowing eyes? None of it made any sense.

With a long exhale, I got out of the car and I let myself into the house. Antonio, my foster dad, was up late playing Xbox with my foster brother in the living room. My greeting went unnoticed by them.

Vanessa was in the kitchen cleaning up after dinner. "Hey, sweetie, how was the beach?" She kissed my cheek. As foster parents went, and I had a lot of experience, these two were the best.

"Okay." I'd told her that we were staying out late with a couple of other friends. Not mentioning anything about a frat party or underage drinking.

She finished loading the dishwasher. "Just okay?"

"Yeah. I have a headache, actually." I turned toward the stairs.

"Wait." Vanessa retrieved an envelope from the counter. "You have a letter."

Probably more college information. I took the envelope from her and glanced at the handwritten addresses. It was an elegant cursive, unlike anything I'd ever seen. Who would be writing to me?

Heading up the stairs to my room, I stopped in the doorway. Even after two years here the room didn't really feel like *mine.* That was no fault of Vanessa's, she'd bought the emerald green comforter just for me. Let me put band posters on my walls. And hang strands of clear lights around the window.

But who knew how many foster kids had lived in it before me. And once I left, another one would come in. In six short weeks, I'd leave all of this behind and move into the dorms at UMBC. No more parents, no more of living in other people's houses.

Though, I would stay in touch with Antonio and Vanessa, at least that was my hope. Even though I was already eighteen and free of the system, moving out was the last step.

While I was excited for the changes, a part of me wanted to stand still, to have this summer last a little bit longer. I was ready to not be a kid anymore, but unsure of whether I was ready to become an adult. To really be on my own. Especially if creeps like the one tonight were waiting for me in college.

At least Elena was coming with me. We'd have each other. Watch each others backs.

I closed the door, leaning against it, and lifted the envelope, studying the unfamiliar handwriting once more before ripping it open. Inside was a letter in the same flourished script.

Dear Caprice,

I hope this letter finds you in good health and happiness. My name is Isabella Sorrentino, and I'm your grandmother; your birth father's mother. I have been searching for years to find you, and am so glad that I finally have.

I would love to meet you. Given my age, travel does not agree with me very well. I live in Oregon and I want to pay for a plane ticket for you, so that you may visit me this summer.

My phone number is written at the bottom. Please call me and I will arrange everything. I so look forward to meeting you and telling you about your family.

All my blessings,

Isabella

My head swam, and I crouched down so that I wouldn't fall over. I had blood relatives—or at least one. A grandma.

I stared at the carpet. My heart pounded, filling my ears with its uptempo beat. Tears moistened my cheeks, and I let them fall. I'd dreamed of this letter for years, mostly when I was younger and filled with hope. But it never came—until now.

Wiping the tears away, I reread the letter. What if she had the wrong Caprice Sorrentino? There was a chance that this was all a mistake and I wasn't the granddaughter she sought. It was never good to be too hopeful.

I read it a third time before folding the letter and setting in on my nightstand.

It was late here, but earlier in Oregon. I pulled out my phone and it lit up with a touch. Almost midnight here, which made it nearly nine in the west. I dialed the number that was written as a post script.

It rang four times, and I chewed the inside of my cheek.

"Good evening, this is Isabella." The woman who answered had a deep, purring voice. She had to be old, to be my grandmother, but she didn't sound old.

I cleared my throat. "Hello, Isabella, this is Caprice. I got your letter."

I told Antonio and Vanessa about the letter and phone call at breakfast the next morning. My foster brother Max was the first one to respond.

"So sometimes families do search for their kids?" he asked.

I didn't want to give him too much hope. As far as I knew his dad was in jail and his mom was an addict. He might have a grandparent looking for him, but chances of that were not great.

With a brief smile, I said, "Sometimes."

Vanessa reached over and squeezed my hand. "You may be eighteen, but you're still under our protection. Before you make any plans, I want to make sure this woman is who she says she is."

I nodded. Fair enough.

"I'll call in a favor and have her checked out." Antonio was a lawyer in the District Attorney's office. "If she's really your grandmother, we'll decide what to do next. Together."

Part of me wanted to tell them that I had this all under control, that I'd already made my plans, and could take care of myself. Two years ago I would have done just that. But this family had changed me. They'd made me realize that I didn't have to do everything myself and that I could trust others—or at least these two and Elena.

Trusting three people in the entire world, that was some serious progress.

Antonio went to work and Vanessa packed up Max for summer camp. I lounged on the couch, thumbing through social media but not really absorbing any of it.

It had ended up being a long talk with Isabella last night. My impression was that she was kind, outgoing, and genuinely interested in knowing me. We made tentative plans for August. She told me the sooner she could book the plane ticket the better. But I'd had to talk with my foster parents first, which she totally understood.

My stomach felt light and bubbly, like it was trying to rise up through my throat and float away. I still couldn't believe that I had a grandma and she wanted to meet me. In one night my whole life had changed.

I pushed down on the sensation that I recognized as hope and excitement. Take it one day at a time. Don't get too consumed by it all. I needed a distraction. I needed to tell Elena.

After a quick text exchange, I got dressed and walked the short distance to Elena's house. I let myself in. Waving to her parents, I jogged up the stairs to her bedroom.

She was an only child, so she had everything. Her room was the epitome of girly-girl decorated in white and pink. It was like living inside a barbie house. Too many frills for me.

For the first time it occurred to me that leaving to live in the dorms was probably going to be harder for her than me. She'd lived here her entire life. What an experience that would be.

"So what's up? Tell me." She sat on her bed, and I joined her.

"This." I handed over the letter.

She read it. Her eyes growing wide. She smiled. "This is great news! I'm so happy for you. I just can't believe it's taken this long."

"I know. I'm still trying to get my head around it." Taking the letter back, I read it again. "What do you think I should do?"

"Is that even a question?" Elena looked at me like I was crazy.

"I guess not. It's just—" I sighed, bringing my legs up and crossing them. "I don't want to be disappointed. What if she's wrong and I'm not her granddaughter?"

"I'm sure she's done lots of research. She had to have gotten your records in order to find you. How many other Caprice Sorrentino's can there be? With your date and place of birth, and who're in the foster system? Like none."

"Right."

Elena threw a pillow at me. "Come on, this is so exciting!"

I smiled. "You're so my cheerleader." Though the words were sarcastic, Elena always encouraged me when I needed it most.

A frown crossed over her delicate Italian features. "What happened last night? At that party? I mean, you told me some, but...what happened?"

I slid the letter into my back pocket. "That guy tried to rape me."

"Oh my God, are you all right?" Elena reached out to take my hand. "We should report him. Call the cops."

I shook my head. "I didn't even get a good look at him. I'd only be able to give them a vague description. And I'm fine. He didn't hurt me. Just freaked me out." For some reason I couldn't explain, I didn't want to go into the details of the mind control and glowing eyes. Plus, he'd said I wasn't human. How freaky was that? My chest clenched. I pushed the familiar feeling of panic back down. Why were his words bringing up this old anxiety?

I shrugged off the feeling. "I think we should be more careful, though. Last night...I feel like I was lucky that it didn't turn out worse."

"Yeah, I totally agree. From now on, we stick together at parties."

"Deal."

"Want to get out of here?" Elena asked.

"Sure." We spent another long day at the beach. The warmth and relaxation helped me to almost forget about last night. It was hard to imagine predators even existing on such a perfect day.

I returned home late. Antonio was waiting up for me in the living room. He motioned for me to come sit on the couch. It was after ten o'clock and Vanessa had already turned in.

I sat down. "What's up?"

"I have some good news for you."

My heart squeezed. I waited for him to continue.

"I looked into your grandma. Her name is Isabella Sorrentino and she is the late Luca Sorrentino's mother. She lives in Estacada, Oregon, which is right outside of Portland. Before she retired, she had a long career as a nurse."

Since it was my grandmother contacting me, I'd figured my birth father was either dead or in jail. Still, the shock of knowing he was gone made my stomach drop.

"So she's legit?" I asked.

"You have the same last name. I know your father's not listed on your birth certificate, so we can't be one hundred percent positive. But, I did see Luca Sorrentino's drivers license picture, and there's no overlooking the family resemblance."

I swallowed the lump wedged in my throat. "Can I go see her?"

Antonio nodded. "Of course you can. But I don't want you to be in her debt, in case anything...happens. So I bought you a plane ticket. You're leaving the first week in August."

I leaned into him and gave him a bearhug. "Thank you! That means so much to me."

He returned the hug, then pulled away. From his suit coat pocket, he pulled out the printed plane ticket information. "Don't lose this." He handed it to me.

"Thank you. Although, I'll pay you back for it some day."

"Don't worry about it, Caprice. Consider it a graduation present. I know that's hard for you, but just accept it. All right?"

"Okay." I stood. "Thanks again. Goodnight." I went upstairs. A mix of excitement and fear swirled in my gut. I really had a grandma. What if she didn't like me?

August was only a couple of weeks away, I needed to think about packing. And what to wear that would make a good impression. I'd ask Elena, she was always much better at that kind of stuff.

I knew she was still awake, so I sent her a text with the good news. We texted back and forth until two in the morning.

The morning of my trip finally arrived. I was filled with the jitters. Elena was on vacation with her family, and Max was still at summer camp, so only Vanessa and Antonio saw me off at the airport.

With Elena's help, I was all packed. She'd made me borrow a couple of her more conservative dresses, just in case grandma was old-fashioned. I was also required to pack a sweater. Apparently it could get cold in Oregon, even in August. I didn't believe that. But whatever.

"Remember," Antonio said, "when you're ready to come home, you call the airlines and set a return date. If you need to come home sooner than that, just call me."

I nodded.

"And check in every Sunday. Just send me or Vanessa a text. Okay?"

I rolled my eyes. "I am an adult, you know."

"I know. But humor me until you're in college."

I hugged him and Vanessa goodbye.

The flight was long. So long. I didn't know it was possible to stay in the air that many hours. We had one short stopover in Denver. Then the plane continued onto Portland, Oregon.

Between Denver and Portland I dozed. The dream snippet was a familiar one—recurring for at least the past several years. I was in a dark room with dirty brown carpet. It was nighttime. The shouting started from downstairs. "Clumsy bitch! Deserves the belt!" Panicked, I ran down the hall to the stairs. In the living room, tears streamed down the face of a little girl. Everything exploded in red.

I jolted awake in the airplane seat. Always the same dream. But what did it mean?

"We'll be landing in Portland, Oregon in twenty minutes." A voice came through the cabin speakers.

When we landed, of course, my sense of time was all messed up. My internal clock said it was ten at night, but the local time was only seven. It was bright and sunny outside, with a temperature of seventy-nine degrees. At least that's what the flight attendant said as we taxied in.

I grabbed my carry-on once the plane had stopped rolling, then shuffled out with the rest of the people. My grandma had said someone would meet me at the gate and drive me to her house. Apparently, Estacada was about forty minutes from the airport.

As I exited the secured section, I searched around for whoever Isabella had sent. She hadn't told me anything about how I was supposed to recognize them.

I scanned the crowd that waited for their loved ones. My gaze fell on the cardboard sign first. It read: Sorrentino. Then my eyes traveled upward to take in a well-built chest, broad shoulders, a square jaw, and piercing grey eyes under wavy blond hair.

Maybe he was here for a different Sorrentino. Because grandma couldn't possibly be associated with a hunk like that, could she?

The man approached. He was a little older than me, my guess was early twenties.

"Caprice Sorrentino?" he asked. My heart fluttered as he said my name.

I cleared my throat. "Yeah. I'm Caprice."

He smiled, extending his hand. "Jaxon McIver." His hand was warm, dry, and strong. I blushed as I shook it, hoping he wouldn't notice my reaction to him. "Welcome to Oregon, Caprice."

3

CAPRICE

I sat in the passenger seat of the SUV as Jaxon drove us out of Portland and into the country. So far we'd chatted about the weather and the differences between the east and west coast, while shooting furtive glances at each other. Damn he was hot.

To avoid staring at him, I gazed out the window. We traveled along a winding river with evergreens and big maples all around.

He broke the silence that had been building between us for the past few minutes. "So, you're Isabella's granddaughter?"

I allowed myself a glance at his perfectly masculine face. "Shouldn't you have made sure of that before you picked me up at the airport?"

He chuckled, a deep rumble in his chest. "I know you're her granddaughter. I was just hoping for some…more information."

"You mean you want the inside scoop?" I continued to look out the window to keep a clear head. Just sitting next to this guy was overwhelming. It was like his presence was too big for the inside of the SUV. It pressed against me, and I was in danger of being swallowed up in it.

"You could say that," he said.

"Well, I've been in foster care since I was three. I really didn't think

I had any other family. Then a few weeks ago, I got a letter from Isabella saying she had been looking for me for years. Now I'm here. How do you know her?" I was most curious about that.

"I'm a family friend. I've known Isabella all my life. She's an amazing woman, I think you'll like her."

The trees gave way to farmland before we entered a town. We drove through a small, dingy downtown area, then out into more trees.

I turned to look behind us. "Was that Estacada?"

"Part of it."

"So she doesn't live in town?"

He shook his head. "Nope. Just outside. We'll be there in a couple of minutes."

We drove on the narrow two lane road as it twisted and turned through the trees, until Jaxon made a right onto a long driveway. At the end was an adorable Victorian style house. Surrounded by an extensive vegetable and herb garden.

Jaxon parked the SUV right in front. "I'll grab your bags." He turned to get out of the vehicle. With each movement his back muscles rippled under the fitted black T-shirt. I caught myself staring after him, snapping my mouth shut.

Never in my life had I been so distracted by a guy—especially a hot one, who was probably secretly an asshole. Although he'd been nice enough on the ride here.

Chewing on the inside of my cheek, I let myself out of the SUV.

The screen door slammed shut, and out walked a short woman with long silver hair. Her curvy figure was clothed in a sundress. She had to be in her sixties, but there was a fun-loving youthfulness in her face and appearance.

"Caprice!" Her husky voice called, as she stretched her arms wide.

I smiled, letting her embrace me. She kissed both my cheeks, then stood at arms length, evaluating me.

Her gaze was kind as it surveyed me from head to toe. Up close, her face showed permanent laugh lines around her mouth and eyes. This was a woman who enjoyed life. Who went with the flow and made the best of any situation. At least that's what I saw in her.

"You are a Sorrentino. Look at you!" Isabella said. "Come, we have much to talk about."

Jaxon followed us into the house. He went up the stairs, my gaze following his easy movements as he carried both my suitcases. Then I turned my attention to the inside of the house.

The place was done up in an elegant style. Polished wood floors were covered with subtle floral-patterned area rugs. Striped wallpaper, gleaming baseboards, high ceilings. All the furniture was wood and upholstery. It was the most magnificent house I'd ever seen.

Grandma Isabella led us into the kitchen where a wall of windows let in the evening light. The aroma of baked cheese and herbs hit my nose. My stomach growled. I'd snacked on the plane, but hadn't had a full meal since breakfast.

"I'm glad you're hungry," she said. "Sit, please."

I sat at the rustic farmhouse table in the middle of the enormous kitchen. Isabella pulled a casserole from the oven, setting it on the stovetop. My mouth watered just looking at it.

Jaxon walked in, and my gaze shifted to him. He stood with his thumbs shoved into his jean pockets, exuding ease and confidence. Yet I sensed some deeper power in him—he was formidable.

"Are you staying for dinner?" Isabella asked.

My stomach erupted in butterflies. Part of me wanted to spend more time with this beautiful man. But another part knew that I'd be too nervous to eat. My food would end up all down my shirt, and it would be a disaster.

Jaxon shook his head. "Not tonight. I need to head home." He approached her, kissing her on the cheek. He turned to me. "It was nice to meet you, Caprice." His grey eyes held mine for a long moment. Then he left.

I mentally kicked myself for freezing up. I'd never been so pulled in by a guy before—actually that wasn't true. The memory of the creep at the beach party sprang up. He'd lured me in with…compulsion? Whatever that was. It had freaked me out. I never wanted to be that easily taken in again. I'd have to keep my guard up around Jaxon, because something about him threatened to lure me in.

Isabella had made Eggplant Parmesan, which was amazingly delicious. I hadn't been very good at contributing to the conversation while we ate. She seemed to recognize that I wasn't being rude, I was just starving.

After dinner there was strawberry ice cream for dessert. We took our bowls to the sunroom, watching the last rays of daylight disappear.

Isabella sat next to me on a rattan daybed. "You must have a million questions for me," she said. "But I'd like to start, if that's okay?"

I nodded, sucking on my spoon.

She set her mostly full bowl of ice cream aside. "I didn't want to tell you any of this over the phone given…the nature of it." Her brow furrowed, her eyes filled with sadness. The happy, easy-going Isabella was gone. This woman looked many decades older, tired, and filled with sorrow.

I let my spoon drop into my bowl. All of my attention on her, as my stomach filled with dread.

"Do you know how your mother died?" she asked.

I swallowed the lump that had formed in my throat. "Yeah. She was mugged and shot." I didn't remember any of it, just the details my case worker had shared with me when I was old enough.

Isabella licked her lips. "Your father didn't know about you until a few years after you were born. Your mother finally sent him a letter, it must have been only a few months before her tragic death. The problem was, she didn't tell him where she was living. He searched, but without any solid information, he couldn't find you. And he had no idea your mother had died, and you'd been gobbled up by the foster system. Since your mother was an immigrant, it was even harder to search for you."

A whole array of emotions warred inside me. For so long, I'd thought he'd left because of me. When in reality, he hadn't even known I'd existed. My stomach twisted with a mix of sadness, relief, and anger at the unfairness of it all.

Isabella continued, "He died when you were about five years old. In a fight with some locals." Her brow creased, she blinked several times, then swallowed hard. "I didn't know about you, or his search for you, until several years after his was gone. That's when I went looking for you."

"How did you find me?" I asked.

"With sheer luck." Isabella snorted. "An old friend of your father's works in the admissions office at University of Maryland Baltimore. When she saw you, she called me. That's how strongly you resemble your father."

I slowly nodded, taking this all in. "Why...why did he leave my mother?"

Isabella's tan face turned a deep crimson. "I hope you will forgive me. Jaxon is a phone call away if you want to leave." She drew in a shaky breath, not meeting my eyes. "It was my fault." Her voice broke. "I didn't think she was good enough for him. I tore them apart. I'm so sorry."

The silence grew heavy between us. I tried to wrap my brain around what she was saying. My father hadn't abandoned us because he'd wanted to. My parents might even have loved each other, but not enough. My life would have been completely different if it weren't for this woman sabotaging it.

When I could finally speak again, I asked, "Why did you think she wasn't good enough?"

"It's so stupid, looking back on it now. But I wanted him to marry an Italian-American. And one of us. When he fell in love with a woman from Cyprus, well..." Her mournful eyes found mine. "Do you wish to leave?"

I shook my head. She may have ruined my life, but she was the only family I had. And, she seemed to feel horrible about what she'd done to me.

"I'm glad you want to stay." She took some bites of half-melted ice cream. "I've set some things in place... in an attempt to make up for what I've done. I know nothing will ever be enough to change the past, but perhaps your future can be happier."

Her lips lifted in a sad smile. "Your father was an only child, so I've made you my heir. I had a good feeling about you, after speaking with you on the phone. I will also be covering your college tuition. Maybe Europe for college?"

I set the bowl down in my lap so I wouldn't drop it. With a few sentences, my entire life had changed. I'd been planning on finding a job so that I could work full-time and attend college, to minimize the amount of debt I'd graduate with.

"I-I can't—you don't even know me," I said. People didn't just give you everything, did they? My mind reeled with the implications of what she was offering. Paying for college? Traveling to Europe?

Isabella smiled, and the warmth was back. "I am very good at reading people, Caprice. You are a good person. I have complete faith in you, and I want you to have my legacy."

Besides this house, I wondered what her legacy included. Was she really rich enough to pay for college outright? In Europe? I felt like I was taking advantage of a remorseful old woman. It didn't feel right.

"You must be tired after such a long day," she said. "Come. I'll show you to your room."

We dropped our bowls off in the kitchen sink, then walked through the dining room to the staircase. Upstairs were four bedrooms and two bathrooms. Mine was in the northwest corner.

The room was tastefully decorated in white and pale green. The two brand new suitcases that my foster parents had bought for me stood near a white-washed dresser. The bed was a four-poster draped in green fabric that matched the curtains.

Isabella stood just inside the door. "I hope this room suits you. Sleep in if you'd like tomorrow, I know the time difference can be a challenge. Good night." She closed the door, leaving me alone.

I fished my phone out of my pocket. It was almost ten here, which meant my internal clock was at one in the morning. Between that, and taking in everything that Isabella had said this evening, I was exhausted.

My phone chirped several times on the nightstand, waking me up. I reached for it. The time read seven in the morning. The texts were from Elena.

How was your flight? What's your grandma like?

Call me when you get this!

Are you awake?

What time is it there?

I groaned, silenced the phone, and rolled over. Because of tossing and turning so much of last night, I'd had like five hours of solid sleep. It always took a while to adjust to new surroundings. For the first few nights in a new place, I never slept deeply.

By the time I got up, at ten, my phone had nearly twenty texts on it from both Elena and my foster parents. Geez, couldn't they wait a minute?

I went to the bathroom and brushed my teeth and smoothed my hair. Feeling a little bit refreshed, I called Antonio first so that he wouldn't freak out.

He answered with, "There you are."

"Yeah. You know it's like three hours earlier over here right?"

"When I didn't hear from you last night, I got a little worried, Caprice. How was your flight?"

"It was fine. Isabella is really nice. She cooked dinner and we talked." I'd fill him in on the details later, once I'd decided what to do with Isabella's offer.

"Good to hear. Well, I won't keep you. Just wanted to make sure you arrived safely. Now call me on Sunday to check in, okay?"

"I won't forget. Say hi to Vanessa and Max for me."

We said our goodbyes and hung up.

I knew the conversation with Elena was going to be much longer. So I sent her a summary text, telling her I'd call a little later. I couldn't wait to fill her in on everything. First though, I needed food.

Making my way down the hall, then down the stairs, the air filled with the smell of pancakes. This grandma was amazing. Maybe a little too perfect with all the cooking. As I neared the kitchen, the aroma intensified and my stomach gurgled.

I hadn't bothered to get dressed yet, so I stepped into the kitchen wearing a new set of satin pajamas. They were black with little pink flowers. And I immediately regretted my laziness.

Standing in front of the stove was Jaxon. He wore those hip-hugging jeans and a black T-shirt, with what had to be one of Isabella's lace-bordered, blue aprons. He flipped pancakes in the air while chatting with my grandma. She sat at the table, already set for three, and stroked the black cat on her lap.

I stood immobile, trying to decide if I should stay or run back up to my room. Unfortunately, Isabella spotted me before I could get my wits in order.

"Good morning, Caprice." She set the cat down and came to give me a hug.

Jaxon turned. His golden hair caught the morning sunlight. He took in my pajamas and bare feet. His intense gaze making me blush. Then, with a wink, he went back to preparing breakfast.

My knees grew weak at that wink. I thought I might collapse, but Isabella led me to the table in time. Jaxon was way too hot for a lazy morning like this. He shouldn't be allowed out into the world until at least noon.

Friend of the family, huh? He had to be Isabella's best friend to show up and make breakfast. And he could cook—that just added to his attractiveness. Wasn't he neglecting his gorgeous girlfriend right now? He had to have one. So where was she?

Isabella sat across from me, leaving the spot in the middle for Jaxon. "Did you sleep okay last night," she asked.

I shrugged. "It's so quiet out here. Not like Baltimore at all."

"We are a ways outside of the city here. It is peaceful. Today I'll show you around."

Jaxon set warmed plates in front of us filled with pancakes and bacon. My kind of breakfast.

I willed the butterflies inside of me to calm down so I could eat. It mostly worked. I focused on the delicious food rather than the hunk sitting next to me. Again, I felt that overwhelming presence from him. It was like power rolled off him in waves, even though he was casually eating and talking with Isabella. Such a mismatch. Was I imagining it?

"Full moon is on Sunday night," he said to her. "We'll have to make the best of it."

Isabella glanced straight at me, but spoke to Jaxon. "Yes. We will. I'm sure it will be fine."

My interest was piqued. "What happens at the full moon?"

They both grew still and quiet. Okay...

Isabella spoke. "The town has a tradition. The August full moon, we treat similar to Halloween. Except instead of going out, we stay in and hide from the evil spirits who roam that night."

I'd never heard of such a thing. What a weird town. I was about to ask a question, when I caught the glance shared between Isabella and Jaxon. They were lying to me. Why lie about the full moon?

4

CAPRICE

My first impressions of Estacada had been wrong. It wasn't as dingy as I'd thought. There was a cute little downtown walking district on Broadway Street. Isabella took me from shop to shop during the afternoon. Still, compared to Baltimore, it was tiny.

Estacada also had that cliche small town feel that everyone knew everything about everyone else. As we strolled, several people stopped to greet Isabella. All the shop owners seemed to know her too. If this were any other town, I'd think she was famous. But here, it just seemed like the normal way of life.

We had lunch at a little cafe along the river. It was a couple blocks away from the downtown district, but the river view was awesome. Just like the languid river, I had a feeling this was a town where nothing much ever happened.

Isabella nibbled on her fish and chips. "Tell me about your foster home," she said.

That was a more serious subject than I wanted to get into, but I supposed I had to talk about it at some point. I wiped my mouth with the napkin, thinking. "Well, there were four homes."

She looked up in surprise. "I didn't realize."

"That's fine. The first one was good, I was there until sixth grade. Then they moved away. The second home was okay, but their lives went to hell and they couldn't keep me. The one after that was not good. We didn't get along." I glanced down at my plate. That had been the one with the fire—and the accusations. "Then the last one has been the best. Really good people."

Isabella reached over, taking my hand. "I'm sorry you had to go through all of that."

She had no idea, and I wasn't going to enlighten her at this point. So I shrugged. There was no changing the past. I was way more interested in my future.

"Did you fit in with the other children?"

"Not really. I was always a loner and outsider. Until I met Elena—she's my best friend."

"Mmm. Did anything strange ever happen to you while you were growing up?" Isabella asked.

"Like...what?"

"Any unexplained phenomenon?"

"Like ghosts?"

"Ghosts, strange occurrences, anything you wished for that suddenly came to you." She lifted her shoulders in a shrug, as if these were normal topics of conversation.

I snorted. "Nope. Definitely no wishes that came true. That is, until I got your letter. I'd wished for that for a long time."

"I've wished for this for a long time, too. I'm so glad you're here." She smiled, the lines on her face deepening.

I chomped on a french fry, working up to my question. "What was my dad like?"

Isabella's smile turned nostalgic. "Your father was a very good man. Very likable. A good leader. Stubborn." She chuckled. "He always had a mind of his own and there was no telling that boy what to do. Most of the time, any way."

"Do I really look just like him?" I asked. She'd mentioned it a few times, but I still had no proof.

"Very much. I'll show you pictures at home. I actually need to take you back home after lunch. I have an errand to run. We'll have dinner at eight. Oh, and tomorrow is supposed to be an exceptionally warm day. I thought we could go to the river."

"Yeah, that all sounds great."

Besides the weird questions and my suspicion that she was lying about the full moon, Isabella was an easy person to hang out with. She wasn't particularly conservative or old-fashioned. And she made me feel like I could be myself—without judgement. I didn't know how she did it. No one had ever made me feel that it was okay to let my guard down. I hoped it wasn't a trick.

Once we were back at the house, Isabella retrieved a framed photo from her bedroom. "This is Luca, your father."

I took it from her, staring into large brown eyes that reminded me of my own. We had the same oval face, and thick, dark hair.

I blinked. There was no room for doubt left in my mind, this man was my birth father.

Isabella's lips curved up. "I need to go run that errand. I'll see you tonight." She left, leaving me in the foyer holding that picture.

I went out to the sunroom, propping the photo on the end table so I could stare at it while I talked to Elena. I thumbed through to her number, and she answered on the first ring.

"Tell me everything," she said.

I laughed at her enthusiasm. "Grandma Isabella is pretty cool. We're getting along fine. And I look just like my birth father." I told her about the small town, the house, everything I'd learned about my family, and then backtracked to the airport.

"Wait. Your grandma sent a hunk to pick you up from the airport?" Elena squealed. I had to pull the phone away from my ear to avoid going deaf.

"Yeah. He's super hot. But there's also something weird about him. I can't explain it really."

"Well try."

"Okay... It's like his casualness is a cover for who he really is. There's this, I don't know, like energy when he's around. It's like he's full of authority or something. I really can't explain it."

"Dude, you have it bad for him. I'm so excited! Just promise to tell me everything that happens."

"Oh, I will. Aren't you on vacation with your parents right now?"

"Yep. It's been chill. Nothing nearly as exciting as you to report."

"Speaking of which, there's more." I told her about Isabella wanting to make me her heir and pay for college.

Elena gasped. "Holy shit! That's so amazing. You said yes right?"

"I don't know. I mean, she hardly knows me and she's throwing all this at me. It seems kind of suspicious—"

"Caprice, please. You're the only family she has. Of course she's going to leave you everything. That's normal. Normal families do that. Nothing suspicious about it."

"I guess I don't know much about normal families." I leaned back on the rattan couch with a sigh.

"Not too late to learn. And I'm the ultimate authority. My family is so normal, they're boring."

"Don't say that. I love your family. And you do too."

"Ugh, mom's calling me. Gotta go. Text me tonight. Bye." She hung up.

Normal. Family. Two words that had nothing to do with my life. Until now.

That night I slept better, and it was easier to get up a little earlier in the morning. By ten o'clock we'd had breakfast, no Jaxon this time, and were out in the gardens. The Victorian house sat on five acres. Two of which had been cleared for house and garden. The rest were dense forest.

Near the edge, I peeked through the trees, just making out the roofline of another house. "That must be your closest neighbor. Who lives there?" I asked.

Without looking up from the strawberries that she was collecting, Isabella said, "Jaxon."

That explained how he'd come over for breakfast. It was like a three minute walk.

"He said he was a family friend."

"He is. Our families have known each other for generations. I went to college with his grandparents."

"Both of them? Which school?" I went back to pulling what I hoped were weeds from a raised bed of tomato plants.

"Just a local college. We all grew up around here." Isabella tossed a strawberry at me, which I caught and popped in my mouth. It was sweet. Perfectly ripe.

I pulled my long dark hair up into a bun. Last night hadn't cooled off too much, and this morning the temperature climbed into the upper eighties. I was really looking forward to being on the river.

Half an hour later we were weaving our way through the garden and back to the house. For a single woman, Isabella had a huge, beautiful garden. She must spend most of every day tending it.

We stepped into the cool, air-conditioned kitchen. I scrubbed the dirt from under my nails in the kitchen sink before going upstairs to change. My clothes were still in the suitcases instead of the dresser. I wasn't sure how long I was staying.

I selected my red bikini and a pair of cutoffs. Once dressed, I slipped on black flip-flops. My hair was piled high in a messy bun. Luckily, I didn't burn, so I never bothered with sunscreen.

With my phone in my back pocket, I went downstairs. Isabella wasn't in the kitchen or dining room. On the other side of the entry foyer was the seldom used living room. I peeked in.

The room was large with a fireplace on the far wall. A couple of couches and several chairs made for a cozy environment. It was the perfect place to curl up in the winter months. Another thought crept into my head: This place could someday be mine. I'd never thought of owning a house before.

I pushed the thought away. Orphans didn't end up with houses like this. Did they? Only a month ago, I was faced with the reality of putting myself through college. I wasn't a good enough student for a scholarship, so it would all be loans and whatever small grants I could go after. My plan was to go for a business degree, get a stable job, and try to build up an okay life for myself.

Now I felt like a princess in a fairytale. I was heir to a castle. My education would be covered. Maybe I could study a subject I really loved instead of business. Like English Literature. That was a dream.

I turned away from the living room, pressing my back against the cool foyer wall. It was too good to be true. I was feeling hopeful, and that was dangerous. No one gave to another without wanting something in return. What did Isabella want from me?

Voices reached me from the front porch. The door opened, and in came Isabella with Jaxon on her heels. Today he wore jean shorts with his black T-shirt. His long legs were muscular, suiting the rest of his build, and sprinkled with golden hair.

When I looked into his face, his eyes weren't on mine. They trailed down my half-naked body, taking in the bikini top and the proud C-cups it concealed. Then his grey gaze swept over my bare stomach, down to the cutoffs, and over my tanned legs.

Plenty of guys had looked me over before, but this felt different. When his eyes met mine there was no humor or flirtation there. Instead they were like steel—hard and serious. The intensity made me want to back away, but I was already up against the wall.

He broke the spell with an easy smile. It changed his face so completely, that for a moment I was caught off-guard. "Hey there, Caprice. Ready to go to the river?"

Isabella had gone up to her room and was just coming back down the stairs.

"I, uh, still need a towel."

"I've got one for you," Isabella said. "Let's go."

I took the back seat for myself in Jaxon's SUV. The weirdness that I felt toward him was gradually wearing off. But I'd never forget his steely eyes. Did he think I was unattractive, or was it something else? I mean there were plenty of girls prettier than me. Especially those tall, beautiful, blond girls. My lips were too big. My legs too short.

Or it could be something worse. Maybe he thought I was an imposter trying to dupe Isabella. They seemed close, so she probably told him about her plans for me to inherit. If I were him, I'd be suspicious too.

I sat quietly in the back, feeling guilty for no reason. I hadn't done anything wrong. Except not coming clean about certain details of my past. But I didn't want Isabella holding my past against me. I wasn't angry at her for tearing my parents apart. Although I could have been, and she trusted me enough to tell me and risk my anger.

I caught Jaxon's eye in the rearview mirror. He was studying me. Not even trying to hide it this time. I squirmed under his scrutinizing gaze, feeling naked and vulnerable. What was with his guy?

Luckily, the ride to the river was over in just a few minutes. When we got out of the SUV, Jaxon was back to his easy-going self, which wasn't going to fool me any longer.

A car pulled in next to us. Two guys got out of the front seats, their attention on Jaxon.

"Hey!" Called the one closest to us. He was tall, with an athletic build. Red hair fell into his green eyes. A light dusting of freckles covered his nose. Below that were the most kissable lips I'd ever seen.

Jaxon hugged the attractive redhead, as another man came around the car. He was equally as hot, but in a completely different way. Short black hair, deeply tan skin, and amber eyes.

After they exchanged a greeting, Jaxon turned to me. "Caprice, meet Liam and Angel."

I shook their proffered hands, trying not to drool or babble. These three could do serious damage to any woman's sense of calm—especially when all together.

"What are you boys up to today?" Isabella asked, hoisting the large tote onto her shoulder.

"We're meeting some friends up the river," Angel said. "You all want to come along?"

"Nah," said Jaxon, "we're going right down here."

I was mildly disappointed that we wouldn't be going with them. Okay, maybe more than mildly.

"See you later then." Angel gave me a wink before turning to leave. And I thought Jaxon's winks here good. Damn.

Liam followed Angel toward the river. I sighed as their mouth-watering forms grew smaller in the distance.

Jaxon chuckled beside me.

My gaze flew to his face. He raised an eyebrow, but didn't say anything. He caught me checking out his friends. How embarrassing.

Jaxon turned away, taking the large tote from Isabella, and led us down to the narrow beach.

Hordes of people floated past is inner tubes and other inflatable river-craft. Families let their children wade into the water as they picnicked on the shore. Jaxon led us a ways down river to a semi-private cove. There Isabella took the tote back, grabbed a beach towel, and situated herself in the sun with a book on her lap.

I couldn't tell if she was trying to leave Jaxon and me alone, or if she was just oblivious to the tension between us.

I got a hold of the other towel, picked a spot, and lay down. Closing my eyes, I focused on the red glow behind my eyelids. A slight breeze rustled the maple leaves. People on the river called out to each other as they drifted past our spot.

I could sense more than hear Jaxon sit down next to me.

"You're quiet today," he said.

My skin flushed and prickled. I felt his gaze, his powerful presence so close to me. I opened my eyes, shielding them with my arm.

"Don't you have a job?" I asked. It sounded like an accusation.

He laughed. The deep, delicious sound sending a shiver through me. "Yes, I have a job. I'm a professor."

I leaned up on my elbows. Maybe that was why he felt like an authority figure. But, still… "Really? Aren't you a bit young?"

"Not for teaching at a two year college." He lay on his side, so close that he could reach out and touch me. But he didn't. "It's more like a specialized preparatory school. I get summers off."

I made a face. I knew teachers got summers off. "Which school is it?"

"Just a little academy a few miles from here. Not well known."

Turning onto my side, I faced him. He was avoiding my question. "What do you teach?"

"History mostly."

"Mostly?"

"Yes, mostly. You're kind of nosy, you know that?" His eyes lit up with mirth, but I knew it was a mask. What was he really doing here next to me?

Over his shoulder, I spotted Isabella. She seemed to be asleep in the dappled sunlight. Her book lay open on her stomach and her sunhat was over her eyes. A soft snore escaped her parted lips.

"I'm going in the water." I stood up, slipping out of the shorts. This time, when I glanced down at Jaxon, there was heat in his eyes. He licked his lips. Maybe he thought I was attractive after all.

The water was cold. Like freaking freezing. I waded in up to my waist, giving my body a moment to adjust to the temperature. The water rippled toward me from the shore and I turned. Jaxon had taken off his shirt and was already up to his thighs in the river.

Jesus Christ! A shirtless Jaxon was a sight to behold. He was all hard, bulging muscles and smooth skin. He ran a hand through his shaggy blond hair. It was like watching a model at a sexy photoshoot. How did his students focus in his classes?

He caught me staring. The muscles in his square jaw worked and the hardness had returned to his eyes. He smirked, but it didn't lighten his energy. Nor did it hide his true emotions.

Then a thought clicked in my mind. He was playing at being the playboy. But it didn't come naturally to him. Why would he do that? What game was he playing?

He dove into the river, resurfacing as a sun-kissed god right in front of me.

"If you go all in," he said, "your body will adjust to the cold sooner."

I stared up, trying to get a read on him.

He stepped closer, towering over me. "You're a special girl, aren't you?"

My heart hammered in my chest at his closeness. "Special? Not really, no."

"Don't play coy." The back of his hand caressed my arm. "You're safe with us—with me." His intense gaze bored into mine. "Now tell me how you're special."

I tried to step back, but he caught my arm. "I'm not. I don't know what you're talking about."

His questions and staring were starting to creep me out. At the same time, his touch sent heat through my body. Talk about mixed messages.

"Stop lying." His grip tightened. "There's something in your past that makes you different from everyone else. You know there is. Now tell me what it is." The playboy facade was gone. In his place stood a serious, demanding man.

The only way he could know about the fire was if he searched through my record. Was that what he was talking about? It was the only thing in my past that set me apart from others. The only weird, horrifying occurrence from my past—and they'd blamed me. I still didn't know why.

A vision flashed before my eyes: Fire exploding from my mouth as I screamed.

Impossible. I shook it off, refocusing on Jaxon.

"There's nothing," I said. "I'm not—"

"Caprice, stop lying to me." He swooped down, picking me up. I held on to his neck even though my first instinct was to push away.

"What are you doing?" I asked.

He didn't respond.

"Where are you taking me?"

Again, no response. His square jaw was firmly set.

Jaxon strode downstream. We reached a spot where a rock cliff hung over the river. He set me on my feet, and took a step back. For a long moment, his evaluating gaze swept over my face. Thirty feet away, people floated with the current. If I screamed they'd hear me.

"Isabella thinks a subtle approach is best," Jaxon said. "I disagree. I need to know what you are, and how powerful you are, right now. I can make some guesses, but that's not good enough. Now tell me."

"I don't know what you're talking about," I said through clenched teeth.

He sighed. "Fine. Let me make this easier for you. What happens when you get angry? When you lose your temper?"

I gasped. He already knew, he just wanted to make me say it. "I don't lose my temper!"

He arched a brow. "Really?"

"Really. And you have no right to question me like this."

"You're wrong." He came at me, making me back up into the cliff. His body mere inches from mine. "I have every right."

My breath grew rapid as heat flooded my face. I knew the signs. Knew that I was getting angry. I took a steadying gulp of air. This intimidating man was not going to make me lose it. I'd worked so hard, for years, to control my temper. The irony of being half-Italian was not lost on me.

"I won't let you make me mad. No matter what you say—"

His mouth came down on mine. He claimed my lips with unfiltered desire. Caressing, parting them with his tongue. His arms wrapped around my waist, pulling me up out of the water and against his hard chest.

Pure pleasure ripped through me. I steadied myself with my legs on either side of his hips. Two thin pieces of fabric separated our bodies. Through his swim trunks, I could feel *him*. Hot and hard.

I jerked my head back, breaking the kiss. He didn't want me. This was all an act.

"What's wrong?" he asked, thrusting his hips suggestively against my core.

I almost moaned. Instead, I unwrapped my legs and shoved at his chest. "Let me go. Now."

He released me immediately.

I searched his face, trying to make sense of him. He stared back with those steely grey eyes. If there had ever been any lust, it had gone.

"You kissed me to make me angry!" I was appalled. With both hands, I pushed him away. What an asshole! I waded back to the shore where Isabella snoozed, grabbed my clothes and shoes, and headed up the trail.

5

CAPRICE

The late afternoon sun heated my bare shoulders. As soon as I got to the parking lot, I slipped into my cutoffs and flip-flops. Reality hit me like a motorboat.

I was thousands of miles from home. Alone.

At least I had my phone. I pulled it out to text Elena or call Antonio. But what could I tell them? Grandma and this hot guy were freaking me out by asking questions about my past? They got a hold of my file and wanted me to admit to starting that fire.

A chill ran up my neck. It had happened when I was sixteen. One minute I was arguing with my foster father, like I'd done so many times before, and the next, the whole house was a raging inferno. No one was hurt, but the house was gone. My foster father blamed me. The investigation that followed was inconclusive. Then I was taken from there and placed with Antonio and Vanessa.

Deep down, I felt guilty. At times I wondered if I had started that fire. Not being able to remember what had happened was bad enough. If I had started it, then that made me a psychotic freak. I didn't want to be that.

I stared at my phone. Maybe I was overreacting. Isabella had every right to know who I was, and all about my past. I'd want to know, if I were her. I'd want to know exactly who I was supporting and planning to leave my house to.

The past scared me. I didn't want to talk about it, or the implications that went with it. But for Isabella, I should suck it up and let her in. Jaxon on the other hand... I sighed. He was probably trying to protect her. Did he sense something dark in me? Something off?

I found the SUV and leaned against it. My future happiness depended on me being courageous in the present. If I continued to hide the fire incident from Isabella, she may decide I was too suspicious and unworthy of being her heir. If I told her about it, she may decide the same thing. I'd take the gamble.

A few minutes later, Jaxon and Isabella emerged from the trail. Her features relaxed in relief at me standing by the car. Jaxon's face was unreadable.

Silently, we piled in and went back to grandma's house.

That night, after dinner, I finally got up the nerve to speak with Isabella. We sat in the sunroom flipping through a Sorrentino family photo album. I didn't just look like my father, I strongly resembled all the Sorrentino's going back several generations.

With a sigh, I closed the book. "I have something I need to tell you," I said.

"Is it why you left the river today?" Isabella really was perceptive.

"Partly," I answered.

Her deep brown eyes focused on my face.

"I...don't like talking about this. But I think it's what you and Jaxon have been asking about." I took a deep breath. "You asked if anything strange happened to me when I was younger. Well something did." I told her the story as I knew it, and about how I didn't really have a clear memory of that evening.

Once I'd finished, she asked, "Why did your foster father accuse you exactly?"

"He kind of freaked out. He kept saying that the fire came from me. My case worker thought he was in shock from losing his house. But..."

"Yes?"

I shook my head. "The way he said it, and the way he looked at me, like I was some monster...it still haunts me." I placed my shaking hands between my knees. "I know this isn't what you wanted to hear from your new-found granddaughter. I might have some kind of delusional mental problem, but I wanted to be honest with you."

This whole time, I'd been trying to not feel hurt by the rejection that I knew was coming. Who could want a potentially dangerous relative? No one.

Isabella drew out one of my hands to hold in hers. "Caprice, I don't want you to feel bad about what happened. You didn't do anything wrong." She smiled at my open-mouthed stare. "Being part of this family...is different. I have a secret to tell you as well." Her soulful eyes lit up. "I'm a witch."

I burst out laughing. "I'm sorry. I tell you that I might be an arsonist and you tell me you practice Wicca. I don't see those as equally disturbing secrets."

She released my hand, patting it. "Not Wicca. That's a religion. I'm a witch. Actually this whole side of your family is. Your father was one too."

"That's cool. There were a few witches at my high school."

Isabella sighed, seeming disappointed in my reaction. "We'll talk about it later."

"No really, that's fine. I could see why you'd want to keep that a secret in a small town like this." I felt so much better now that we were talking openly. I yawned. "Thank you for not holding my past against me."

"You should get some sleep, dear." She gave me a hug, then let me go upstairs.

Sunday morning, Isabella had a meeting that would last most of the day. I called Antonio to tell him everything was okay. I still didn't know how long I was staying. Then Elena and I talked for a couple of hours. Which was what I needed, because Jaxon was driving me crazy.

"So he runs hot and cold?" Elena asked.

"That and…this whole playboy persona one moment, then it's like a switch, and he turns into this serious, powerful, demanding…man. I just can't figure him out."

"Hmm… Maybe he likes you, but he's trying to pretend that he doesn't. He is a teacher, he could get into trouble." Elena sighed. "Maybe you should give the guy a break."

"Hey, you're supposed to be on my side. Not his." I leaned into the feather pillows, still in my pajamas. "But you could be right. I'm overanalyzing."

"Ha! That's not a first."

I rolled my eyes.

"I felt that eye roll," Elena said.

"Whatever. You can't see me."

"No. But I know you better than you know yourself."

That was probably true, although I wasn't going to admit that to her. "So…any hot guys in Florida?"

"Hell yeah." Elena gave a detailed description of her encounter with a nineteen-year-old from Chicago. All I could think about was that kiss with Jaxon. I'd been kissed before, but not like that. The memory made me squirm. Had he really done that to make me mad? I could be wrong about that too. Although he hadn't denied it.

Around noon, I got off the phone to forage for food. There was leftover casserole in the refrigerator and I helped myself. After eating, I dressed and explored the rest of the house.

On the main floor, behind the living room, was a small library. The walls were floor to ceiling bookcases. In the middle were two lounge chairs on either side of the window seat. The wall that connected to the living room held a fireplace.

I browsed the book selection. Eclectic was a fitting description with titles ranging from obscure to ancient to contemporary. My second foster mother had been a librarian, so I recognized more of these books than most people would have.

One shelf was all dictionaries. I always found the different types and editions interesting to look at. I pulled out one thick volume that had marbled paper. As I slid it from the shelf, a creaking sound made me jump.

To my right, part of the bookcase had...opened. I replaced the dictionary, then gripped the side of the wooden case and pulled. This whole section was a hidden door. I swung it wide.

Inside, polished stone stairs led down into blackness. My pulse rushed in my ears. This was the kind of thing you find and regret—at least in the movies. What was hidden down there? Where did it lead?

Before I could take action on the temptation to explore, the front door slammed shut. Isabella was home.

The bookcase smoothly closed with a slight tick as it locked.

From the foyer, Isabella called, "Caprice? Are you up there?"

I emerged from the library. "In here."

"Find anything interesting?" She studied me for a moment.

"Lots." My heart pounded against my ribcage. No way was I going to admit to finding a secret door in her library.

Isabella hung up her hat and tote. "Tonight is the full moon. It's traditional to lock all the doors and windows." She faced me. "Will you help me secure the house?"

"Uh...sure." This town was wacky.

"You can start with the library, then move clockwise from room to room. I'll get the upstairs."

I turned back in to the library, making sure the one window was locked. Isabella's seriousness about this tradition sent a shiver through me. What did she expect would try to get into the house tonight? Did it know about the secret staircase in the wall?

We had a delicious dinner of two savory quiches followed by mango ice cream. The entire time, Isabella seemed distracted. She kept glancing out the kitchen windows. Once the full moon rose over the ridge, her brow furrowed and stayed that way.

I swallowed the last spoonful of dessert. "You okay? Seems like there's something on your mind."

She waved away my concern. "Nothing for you to worry about. The meeting I attended earlier is still on my mind. But, that's not for you to worry about." Now she was repeating herself. "It's time for bed, don't you think?"

"Sure. Goodnight, grandma."

She kissed my cheek. "I like that you call me that."

I meandered up the stairs, then down the hall to my room. I wasn't particularly tired, so I sat in bed reading a novel I'd taken from the library. One of my goals was to read all of the classics. I'd made it through Salinger, Tolstoy, Dumas, and a few from Austin. The Bronte sisters too, of course. Given the creepy vibe in this house tonight, I decided to start *Frankenstein* by Mary Shelley.

Reading. It might be my only talent.

As the old clock on the nightstand ticked, eleven at night turned into one in the morning. I yawned. Time for bed. I set the book aside, stood, and went to my suitcase on the bench by the window.

That full moon was bright. It cast an eerie golden-red glow over Isabella's garden. The shadows a deep black along the southern side. Except one of the shadows was moving. I leaned closer to the window, squinting. Someone was out there in the garden. They were pulling up plants in one of the raised beds.

I slipped my flip-flops on. It was probably some kid playing around in the full moon. Vandalizing. Whoever it was, they were trespassing and I wasn't going to let them ruin Isabella's garden. She'd put too much work into it for that to happen.

In the hallway, I stopped to knock on Isabella's bedroom door. I tapped lightly with my knuckles. No response. I tried again. Still nothing. She must be a deep sleeper.

I jogged down the stairs, through the kitchen, to the sunroom door. For the first time, I noticed that it had three deadbolts on it—all locked. Which was ridiculous because the whole room was made of glass.

Before unbolting the last one, a moment of unease twisted my stomach. Was this a dumb move? Isabella had never explained what this tradition was all about. If it were *that* important, she would have explained, right?

Which was worse? Breaking some weird small town tradition or letting that person ruined her garden? I wasn't really a superstitious kind of person. I made the practical decision: Rescue the garden.

The door swung open on well-oiled hinges. I closed it behind me, peering out into the sea of raised garden beds. Four steps down, and I was on the ground. Gravel crunched under my shoes.

I walked around the side of the house to where my bedroom window looked out. That was where I'd seen whoever was out there. And there on the ground lay the uprooted plants. What kind of jerk-face would do that?

I strained to listen for footsteps, or any sign of where they were in the garden. The moonlight made it almost impossible for them to hide. I chose a row at random and tiptoed down it. The tall trellises obscured my line of sight. Once I reached the end, I rounded the corner and strode down the next row.

The early morning air was cool against my bare arms and legs. A slight breeze rustled the vegetation, all else was quiet. Abnormally quiet, like a hush had fallen over the world.

Several rows over, the gravel sprayed into the air, as if someone was running along the path. I spun in time to see a huge black shape dart behind another trellis. That was no child. It could be a teenager playing tricks.

"Who's there?" The beating of my heart filled my ears. If it was a teenager, they were larger than me. "You're trespassing. Get out of here!" For the first time, I wished I'd brought a weapon. Even a shovel would have been fine.

Silence. They had to be hiding just out of sight. Slowly, I moved toward that garden path, listening for them to run away. No one moved.

I inched forward to peer around the corner. Nothing.

I placed my hands on my hips, frowning. How could they just disappear like that? I was sure it was this row that they'd ran down. With a sigh, I turned back toward the house. Maybe they'd already left.

A massive body slammed into my back, knocking me to the ground. The skin on my knees and palms burned from the impact. I twisted my head around to look at my attacker.

No one was there.

What the hell? I leaped to my feet, brushing gravel from my shaking hands. Someone had tackled me and run off so quickly that I didn't see them. How was that possible?

Without warning, the same body hit me from the side and sent me sprawling. A masculine chuckle filled the still air.

I crawled backward. My head twisting in every direction, trying to spot the man. I blinked, and he appeared in front of me. No one could move that fast. But as I took him in, that became the least of my worries.

He was tall and broad, dressed in a long black duster. His eyes shone with a golden light that was not a reflection of the moon. It emanated from within him. Long, greasy hair clung to his brutish face.

As he squatted down to gaze at me, the scent of sweat and blood hit my nose. He reached out with a beefy hand, wrapped it around my neck, and stood. My feet dangled. His grip cut off my air supply. I couldn't scream.

He opened his mouth, showing elongated canines and pointed teeth. A gurgling sound escaped my throat. He drew my face closer to his. He sniffed my hair. His tongue darted out, licking my cheek.

Fear held my body in shocked paralysis. All I could do was grab the hand that squeezed my throat with both of mine. My face felt tight, hot from the blood trapped in it. Soon, I was going to pass out. This creature would devour me and leave the remains of my body in this garden.

My vision blurred. I needed air.

A loud metallic ringing signaled my release. I fell for half a second before hitting the ground hard. Pain shot through my shoulder and hip. I drew in breath after breath, holding my neck. Then strong arms lifted me, cradling me against a warm chest.

I knew who it was immediately. Jaxon smelled like spice and oatmeal soap.

He adjusted me so that he had one free hand. I felt his muscles move as he threw something hard at the ground. A moment later we were consumed in bright purple smoke.

I coughed and sputtered. When my vision cleared, we were no longer in Isabella's garden. Tall stone walls met a wooden roof over head. Candle lit sconces cast a dim light on rows of pews. A church?

Jaxon sat down on one of the long wooden benches with me in his lap. He brought his hand up to touch my face and neck.

"Are you okay?" he asked, stroking his thumb along my tortured windpipe.

I blinked up at him. "What just happened?" My voice came out raspy and thin. "What was that thing? Was there smoke?"

"Shh." He moved his thumb to my lips. "You're safe now," he said, but there was doubt in his eyes.

I jerked awake, for a second thinking that I'd had the most bizarre dream. But I was lying on a hard floor, my back pressed against a warm chest, with a muscular arm draped over my waist. I sat up, twisting to look into Jaxon's face. He stared up at me.

We were in a church, laying in the aisle. My hand flew to my neck.

It felt sore, bruised. It hadn't been a dream. It was a nightmare. A living nightmare. My head filled with a billion questions.

Jaxon eased up onto his forearm, his other arm still on my waist. "That's going to take a while to heal."

"What the fuck is going on around here?" The words come out of my damaged throat in a growl.

"You shouldn't have been outside tonight." His eyes hardened. "You have no idea what kind of trouble you're—we're—in now. All we can do is wait until morning, and to hear from the Council."

"What are you talking about?!" I wanted to scream at him, but my voice refused to get that loud.

He sat up, facing me. "We're witches."

"I already know that. What does that have to do with anything?"

"It has everything to do with everything!" His voice echoed in the cavernous space. In a more modulated tone, he continued, "I just told you I'm a witch. Why aren't you freaking out? Or did you already do that with Isabella?"

"Look, it's not that big of a deal. I've been in the witchy shops, I know what it's all about."

He let out an abrupt laugh. "You have no idea what I'm talking about."

I tilted my head to the side in question.

"Not those kinds of witches. We're...supernaturals. Remember that purple smoke right before we arrived here?"

I nodded.

"That was a teleportation spell."

"Bullshit," I said. Did he think this was some elaborate Dungeons and Dragons game?

He gripped my chin, his face an inch from mine. "How do you think we got here? What do you think attacked you?"

"I don't remember how we got here." I wrenched free. "Some psycho attacked me. I'm going to call the police." I searched my pockets. My phone was in my bedroom.

"That was a Tromara vampire, Caprice." Jaxon's voice was flat, matter-of-fact.

A what? I wanted to say bullshit again. Except I'd seen my attacker, and yeah, vampire. He moved way too fast for a human, glowing eyes, sharp fangs, that smell of blood. I shook my head. What was I thinking? Vampires didn't exist.

"You're sick. You know that?" I moved to stand up. Jaxon caught my arm, yanking me back down.

"You've caused enough trouble for one night. You're not going anywhere."

I bared my teeth in a primal expression. "What are you going to do? Trap me here for the rest of the night?"

His warm breath caressed my face. "You're already trapped, cupcake. And you didn't even see the snare."

6

CAPRICE

Faint sunlight poured in from the windows. The church doors opened wide, and half the town must have walked in, taking seats on the pews. I sat in the last row, wrung out from a long night. Jaxon sat next to me, his features set into hard lines. He hadn't left my side since we arrived there.

I watched the crowd pour in. Why were they here on a Monday morning?

Isabella appeared among them, coming straight for me. "Caprice, you're okay." She gave me a hug. "You need to come with me."

"Where? What's going on?" I was so confused by what I'd seen and experienced last night. Jaxon was serious about vampires and witches and supernaturals. And yet...this couldn't be happening.

Isabella took my hand. "Last night...was my fault. I should have told you how important it was to stay inside, but I didn't want to scare you away." Her brow furrowed, her eyes filling with sadness. "Jaxon, thank you. I owe you—"

"No. You know the rule." His face softened. "But, you're welcome."

"We're all in trouble. We'll bear it together," she said. Isabella pulled my hand. "Come with me."

I let her lead me to the front of the church, where four men and two women stood facing the congregation. She pulled me up the steps with her.

"Um, why am I up here?" I whispered to her. "What's going on?" I eyed the hushed crowd. Their attention was fully on us, which made me nervously pick at my nails.

Isabella stood me next to the alter, then turned her attention to the room. "This is my granddaughter Caprice Sorrentino. She made a grave mistake by going outside last night, but it was my fault for not telling her the consequences."

Murmurs rose in the crowd.

"So I will tell her now, with all of you as witness, to make her believe." Isabella half-turned toward me. "Caprice, I'd like you to meet the Supernatural Council." Each of the six inclined their heads as Isabella said their names. "Councilors Gladys McIver, Diego Cortez, Mia Chang, Demarcus Freeman, Linus Steward, and Richard Aimes."

The name McIver caught my attention. Was that woman a relative of Jaxon's? In a town this small they must be related.

She continued, "We rule over this community and keep it safe. A long time ago there was a war within the supernatural community. To end that war, we made a Truce with our enemy, the Tromara. Part of that Truce is to not go out on the night of the August full moon. Anyone who is outside and caught will fall prey to the Tromara."

I stared, blank-faced at my grandma. This had to be a hidden camera joke. Right?

"How is she alive?" someone asked.

"Yeah, why didn't they take her?" Another voice spoke.

"She shouldn't be here," muttered a woman in the front row.

And all of these people were in on the joke. I glanced around the church to find the recording device. Any moment now someone was going to bust up laughing. This was well-planned, and such a group effort. Even that *vampire* had to be in on it.

Isabella faced the room again. "Last night, not only was she outside and caught, but Jaxon fought off the Tromara."

The crowd gasped. Several turned to look at Jaxon in the back row. His face paled. He avoided their eyes.

I placed a hand on my hip. He was in on it too, of course.

One of the council members, the Cortez guy, asked Isabella, "What do they demand as penance for this? Have they come to see you yet?"

Isabella nodded. Her voice sounded strangled. "They demand Caprice."

I couldn't take it anymore. "Come on," I said to her. "This is a joke. I know it is. You guys can stop acting now."

She grabbed both my arms, hard. "Caprice, this is not a joke. Do you remember what attacked you last night?"

I shuddered. "Yeah, but it wasn't a vampire. I mean not really. Right?" She was scaring me.

"Worse than a vampire! A Tromara vampire." Her eyes blazed with desperation. "They're cannibals, Caprice. They eat people!"

I felt the blood drain from my face. She wasn't kidding. This wasn't a joke. Holy shit.

Cortez and the others on the dais stared at us.

"Then we will have to hand her over," he said.

Isabella released me. "I disagree, Diego. She has a right to go through the Academy first."

Diego Cortez shook his head. "That's true, but it's still playing with fire to make demands on the Tromara."

Were they seriously debating whether or not to hand me over to *cannibals*? I stood in stunned silence. My mind not able to fully grasp the situation, no matter how hard I tried.

"I know. But you know why I have to do it." Isabella brought her fists to her chest. "I only just found her. After all these years."

Diego sighed. "I understand. But this could cause trouble for all of us. We must vote." He glanced at the other five leaders beside him.

"Raise a hand for supporting Isabella and demanding the Academy alternative."

Three of them raised their hands. Including Isabella.

"And those in favor of giving Caprice to the Tromara now?" Councilors McIver, Chang, and Aimes lifted their hands.

I gaped at them. Then realized that Diego was the tie-breaker. But which way would he vote?

The sea of people before us leaned forward, waiting for his decision.

"I'm with Isabella," he said, his voice echoing through the church.

A whoosh of air escaped Isabella's lips. "Thank you. I will meet with them tonight to inform them of our decision."

My brain finally got up to speed on what was happening. "You all are telling me that you're supernaturals? Not normal people?" I asked.

Diego answered. "Yes, we are. Everyone in this room is either a witch, shape-shifter, vampire, fae, or werewolf."

"And you are a witch too," Isabella said, reaching for my hand.

I jerked away from her, horrified. "No I'm not! And you're all crazy!" Pushing past the leaders, I sprinted down the aisle, past all these freaks, toward the only exit that I could see. I was almost to the double doors when muscular arms wrapped around me.

I kicked Jaxon in the shin. He let out a pained grunt, tightening his hold. Then, just like last night, the air around us filled with purple smoke. I coughed, struggling to get free.

When the air cleared, we stood in my room at Isabella's house. My eyes widened in horror.

"Believe me now?" Jaxon asked.

I shoved toiletries into my suitcase while Jaxon stood by the door. He kept snapping his fingers, making a flame appear. He'd let it go out, then repeat the process like he was playing with a lighter. After I got past the initial shock, I had to admit it was pretty cool. Not that I was going to tell him that.

Glaring at him, I went back into the bathroom for the rest of my stuff.

"You can't leave, Caprice." His voice sounded tired. Snap, flame, flame gone.

"Watch me." I zipped the case closed. "I'm not a witch. I'm not like you."

He folded his arms over his tight T-shirt. "Yes, you are. You're afraid. Because of what happened to that house. How it went up in flames."

"Does Isabella tell you *everything*?" I mirrored his posture. "And how dare you accuse me of setting that fire! I didn't do it."

"Yes you did. It's as easy as this." He snapped his fingers to produce the flame.

I took in a deep breath. "You're saying I snapped my fingers and burned down my foster father's house?"

"Well, you were angry, so it was probably a little different. But essentially, yes, that's what I'm saying. And that's why you need to stay. To learn how to control your magic."

I sat on the bed, burying my face in my hands. This couldn't be happening to me. The guilt I always carried about that house fire threatened to swallow me whole. What if I was actually dangerous?

"Caprice..?" Silently Jaxon had crossed the room, and was standing right next to the bed. I finally understood what I felt in his presence. That power emanating off of him was actual magic. Magic. It was too much to take.

"Leave me alone."

"Caprice."

"I want to be alone right now."

He heaved a sigh, but left, closing the door behind him. The room felt spacious again, light and airy.

I sat there for a long time. Jaxon and Isabella were witches. They thought I was too. Half the town, at least, were supernatural. There was a Supernatural Council. A vampire had attacked me last night.

I brought my hands up to cover my mouth. Oh God, that guy at the beach party, he had to be...something. He'd said I wasn't human. He wanted to know what I was, because compulsion didn't work on me...

Fuck. I flopped onto my back. This was real. It was all real.

My first impulse was to call Elena. But how could I tell her all of this crazy stuff? No way would she believe me. Would she?

I pulled out my phone, staring at the black screen. I was afraid. Afraid that she wouldn't believe me, and I'd be all alone in this.

A knock came at my door. "Caprice, may I come in?" It was Isabella.

"Yeah." I set the phone down.

She entered, giving me a sympathetic look as she sat down next to me. "Oh, my poor girl. I know this is a lot for you to understand. I wanted to move forward slowly with this, but now everything's changed."

"I don't understand anything. Who are you people? Why am I stuck here?"

Isabella glanced down with a sigh. "I'm one of the seven ruling council members. My family has had a seat on the Supernatural Council for generations—first the European Council and then the one here. We decide on everything in the community. And, we keep the Truce with the Tromara. This is very important to us, because without the it those vile beasts would destroy us all." She touched my cheek. "I don't want to lose you, like I did your father."

"They killed my father?"

"Yes." She let her hand drop. "Every other generation or so, the supernaturals rise up against the Tromara. It always ends in tragedy for us."

"I'm sorry. I didn't mean to cause problems. I...didn't know." I frowned. "Jaxon attacked that thing. He shouldn't have done that, right?"

"That's right. His actions could have broken the Truce. But, they are willing to forgive him. The Tromara want you instead. Of course, I won't let them have you." She finished quickly.

I licked my dry lips. "Why do they want me?"

"Supernaturals can sense and smell the power in others. My guess is that vampire Tromara sensed the magic in you." Isabella grimaced.

"There's no way you can fight that thing. How will you stop them from taking me?" I stood up, pacing the room. "Maybe I should leave. I can go home. That should put plenty of distance—"

"You can't run from them. They'll hunt you down. There is a clause in the Truce that states that a young supernatural has the right to attend the Academy before being taken. And can only be taken if they fail the Academy."

"What Academy?"

"A school for supernaturals. The only one in the United States." Isabella frowned. "I was hoping they wouldn't know about you, and that I could send you to Europe. It's...too late for that now."

"So the Tromara aren't in Europe?"

"No. Only here. And that clause in the Truce is the best we can hope for."

"Why would they agree to a loophole like that?"

Isabella stood. "Because it keeps the balance."

I lifted a brow. She didn't elaborate.

"I will know more tonight. Now come down and have some breakfast."

So many questions bubbled up in me as we walked down the stairs. "Are you all immortal?"

"No. But we do live longer than humans." Isabella poured us each a bowl of cereal, adding fresh berries. "Once we reach the age of twenty-one, the supernatural aging sets in, slowing down the process. I'm almost a hundred and fifty years old."

My eyes widened. "For real?"

"For real." Isabella set the bowl in front of me at the table. "The

Tromara, however, are immortal. Besides cannibalism, it's what sets us apart."

I nodded while chewing on crunchy corn flakes, giving my brain a chance to adjust to all this...freaky shit.

Late that night, Isabella returned. I was waiting for her in the living room, trying to read my book. But my mind kept drifting to everything that had happened in the past few days.

When she walked in, I slapped the book shut and set it on the table. "Well?" I asked. My fate was about to be revealed. I was feeling kind of impatient—anxious. Terrified.

"They've agreed." She let her long silver hair out of its clip.

"Why don't you seem happy about that? I'm safe now, right?"

"I won't lie to you, Caprice. The Academy is designed so that a certain number of students will fail every year."

I recoiled. "What kind of school does that?"

"One set up to keep the Truce alive and well." Her lips turned down. The lines in her face seemed deeper than usual. "I'm tired. Try to get some sleep. We'll worry about school when September gets here."

September was only a few weeks away.

That Sunday, I called Antonio, then Elena. He took the news that I was going to live with my grandma and attend school in Oregon as if it wasn't that big of a surprise. I told him Isabella was going to adopt me too. Which he was genuinely happy to hear. Vanessa would make arrangements to ship the rest of my belongings out here. They wanted me to visit next summer, and in the meantime keep in touch.

Elena took the news as I'd expected.

"You're ditching me? After everything?" Elena's voice was higher pitched than usual. "We made plans, Caprice. We're supposed to go to college together, remember?"

"I know. But that was before I found out I had family. I want to stay close to her and get to know her."

"I can't believe you're ditching me! Can't you just go visit her on holidays?"

"No. I can't. She's my grandma. I don't know how long she'll live. And she's the only family I've got."

"I get that. I do. It's just...we had plans. We had plans for our lives."

"I know. I'm sorry, Elena." I was so tempted to tell her why I had to stay. That there were freaking supernatural bad guys who wanted to eat me, and this school was my only chance to live. But I couldn't tell her. Partly because I was afraid. Partly because I didn't want her to get involved with any of this, and the less she knew the better.

When we hung up, I felt awful—hollow. I'd had to start over several times growing up, but these people I trusted and loved. Yet, here I was, starting over again.

For the rest of August, I didn't see Jaxon, although I knew he was next door. Some days I was tempted to walk over there and talk to him. But I'd almost gotten his family and friends in trouble with those cannibals. He probably hated me for that. I couldn't blame him.

Isabella let me change some things in my room to make it fully mine. I hung my favorite band posters on the walls, installed some mood lighting, and added some color to the space with new rugs and pillows. I'd live here in the summer. The rest of the year I'd be at the Academy.

A few times I'd gone into Isabella's library searching for the book that opened the secret room. I'd tried all the dictionaries, but none of them opened the door in the wall. Defeated, I gave up.

The warm August days turned cooler as soon as September arrived. Three days before school started, Isabella drove us into Portland to find a witchy supplies store. Her favorite was in the southeast area.

I slammed the car door shut, studying the single story witch shop in the busy shopping district. "Are we really going to find what we need here?" I asked Isabella. I still hadn't accepted that I was a witch, not really. Maybe this school would awaken my magic.

"Everything except a couple of school books and your wand. You'll get those on campus." She opened the door and a bell chimed. "We do use normal things like herbs, crystals, candles, and such."

"Good to know," I murmured, following her in.

The shop was long and narrow. At the front were displays of crystals, magical sprays, and other supplies. The back half held rows of book shelves.

"Welcome in," called the twenty-something hipster from behind the sales desk.

I sidled up to Isabella. "What are we looking for exactly?"

"Herbs mostly. You'll need them for potions."

Potions. Right. This all still sounded completely crazy.

Against one wall were a hundred glass jars filled with dried herbs. Isabella went to work measuring and bagging about twenty of them, as I wandered the rest of the shop.

A circular table with little bowls of stones drew my attention. I picked up a tumbled black piece, rolling it around in my palm. The sign said it was black onyx, used for protection. No wonder I was attracted to it. I chewed my bottom lip. Could this little stone really protect me?

The doorbell chimed, and I glanced in that direction. My breath caught. Jaxon walked in, his arm around an absolutely gorgeous woman. She had long strawberry hair, green eyes, and the perfect smattering of freckles across her nose. I hated her instantly.

Jaxon said hello to Isabella, then turned his attention to me. "Caprice, I want you to meet one of your teachers." He waved to the beautiful woman. "This is May. She'll be your potions teacher."

I shook her hand, plastering on a fake smile.

"Got everything you need for school?" Jaxon asked me, his grey eyes warm and soft. As if he hadn't been avoiding me for weeks.

"I don't know." I turned to Isabella. "Do we need anything else?"

She glanced at the list in her hand. "Ah, one book. *Mythology Around the World.*"

"I know right where that one is," Jaxon said, moving toward the back of the store.

Not knowing what else to do, I followed him. He was such a player. I should have known that as soon as I met him. A man that good looking couldn't be anything else. Of course he'd spent the past few weeks with his girlfriend instead of me.

At the far back corner, Jaxon reached up to the top shelf for the mythology book.

I folded my arms. "So, you have a girlfriend?"

"She's not my girlfriend." He studied the title page. "Just a fellow teacher."

Like I was going to believe that for a second. "You flirted with me, even though you have a girlfriend. Don't you think that's wrong?"

"Not really, since she's not my girlfriend. Not that it would matter if she were."

My brows drew together. "What?"

"I flirted with you. But it didn't mean anything. I needed information." He held out the book. I didn't take it.

"What do you mean?" My heart beat faster as dread swirled in my stomach.

When he looked at me, his eyes were steely. "I've found that sexual energy is the quickest way to get close to someone. I needed to know who you were, and I didn't have a lot of time."

My mouth dropped open. "You led me on? You...bastard!" I shouldn't have been so surprised, I knew he was a player. But him admitting it, as if there was no chemistry between us at all, in that casual tone, was infuriating.

"I did what I needed to do." He dropped the book into my hands. Brushing past me, he disappeared around a bookcase.

I took in deep breaths to calm the fury bubbling up in me. No wonder he'd avoided me these past few weeks. He got what he wanted. That was it. He was done with me.

Swallowing hard, I rubbed my face, trying not to cry. I'd been such an easy mark, responding to everything about him. His closeness, his scent, his kiss. I wouldn't make that mistake again—ever.

7

JAXON

"I can't believe you said that to her, Jaxon." Liam sat next to Angel on the front porch couch.

I took a swig of my beer. "It's the truth. Besides, I couldn't have her hanging all over me at the Academy."

Half of Angel's mouth lifted in a smirk. "Excuses. That's all I hear."

Angel had an annoying way of getting to the truth of the matter, especially when I didn't want him to. Was I making excuses? What I'd said to Caprice was unforgivable. If I were her, I'd be furious right now. And I'd never want to see me again.

The tightness in my chest wouldn't let go. It had been there ever since I'd come up with my plan to distance myself from Caprice. The past three weeks had been hell. She'd been so close, living next door, yet so out of reach.

At first, playing the suave charmer had been easier than I'd thought it would be. I had to vet Caprice, for all our sakes, but especially for Isabella. But, then Caprice...well, she was more than I'd thought she'd be. Or maybe I was just a sucker for foster kid sob stories.

No that wasn't it. I liked her strength, how she held her own against me. She was sexy but didn't know how much she affected me. I liked how brave, smart, funny--yeah…I couldn't fall for her. Out of the question.

"I don't see why she even likes you," said Angel. "You're all serious and brooding, man. Not attractive."

Liam rolled his eyes. "Not all women like smart-asses like you."

Angel spread is arms wide, still holding his beer bottle. "Show me one who doesn't. I'm a love magnet."

"I'm sure she doesn't like me anymore. I did a good job of ending that." I raked a hand through my hair.

Liam said, "I still don't know if that was the best course of action."

"Yeah, man, how are we supposed to make sure she doesn't fail the Academy when she thinks we're all assholes because we're friends with you? Did you think of that?" Angel gulped down the rest of his beer. I did the same.

Fuck. I hadn't thought of that.

"We'll figure it out," Liam said, swirling his IPA. "Isabella's heir needs to survive. She needs to take her place on the Council one day if the Sorrentino line is going to survive."

"If it weren't for Isabella, I'd say fuck the Sorrentinos. Let the UK witches take over the seat." Angel got another bottle from the cooler he'd brought.

"I'm not taking the place of Isabella or Caprice." My jaw tightened. United Kingdom witches versus Italian witches, it was an age old war. A war that had come to an end several generations ago. I wasn't going to revive it.

Although my aunt would be perfectly happy if I did. Gladys McIver had stepped up to fill my father's role on the Council after he died, when I was a child. But since that seat was an inherited one, it was mine by right. When I finally decided to take it.

Angel shrugged. "Scottish. Italian. Makes no difference to me."

Liam pursed his lips. "She'll be in my class this term. I'll keep an eye on her—"

"She's in my class too," I said.

"What are you thinking?" Liam set the bottle down too hard. "Jaxon, you burned that bridge. Leave her alone. Angel and I will take over looking out for her."

"No." I shook my head. "It'll be fine. I promised Isabella."

Liam gave me a dubious glance. "I'd argue with you more, but you're a stubborn son of a bitch. Fine. Have her in your class. She can come running to me the next time you piss her off."

I growled.

"You know what I'm saying is true." Liam settled back with a sigh. "I'm the most qualified to look after her emotional health, and you know it."

Sometimes I wished I had the emotion reading ability unique to the fae, then I remembered how Caprice hated me and was glad that I didn't. She could turn to Liam for comfort. It didn't matter.

My chest clenched tighter with jealousy. I pushed away from the railing, grabbed another beer, and popped the top off with the opener that lived on the windowsill.

Angel spoke up. "I don't care about her *emotional health*. See, using words like that, that's why you never get laid, man."

Liam glared at him, but the tops of his ears turned pink.

"What I care about is why those Tromara bastards didn't take Jaxon's head for rescuing the girl. My dad thinks you're real lucky. What do you guys say about that?"

I hid my face with a long swig. Rescuing her from the Tromara vampire had been the single most stupid thing I'd done in my life. It was part of the reason I knew I had to distance myself from Caprice. Another mistake like that could lead us all to war—again. All the lives lost in that war would be my fault. And the scary part was I'd rescue her again in a heartbeat.

I didn't want to be like my father. It was hard enough being the son of the last rebellions leader. Everyone knew I was a bad seed, just waiting to sprout. The only three people who thought differently were Isabella and these two sitting on my couch.

"They want her, obviously," Liam said, "but they don't want us to know how badly they want her. By not punishing Jaxon, they're trying to make us think she's not desirable to them. But by them acting all nonchalant about it, tells me they are up to something big and bad."

Angel shook his head. "I don't think the Tromara are that smart."

"Don't underestimate them," I said. "I agree with Liam. They are biding their time. For what I don't know. Nothing good."

"Why do you think they want her?" Angel asked. "What's so special about her?"

I didn't have an answer to that. I knew why she was special to me. But what had that Tromara vampire sensed in her? That fucker had *licked* her. My fist clenched at the memory.

All we could do was watch her closely at the Academy, help her to succeed, and keep her safe from the Tromara. Between the three of us, we had this. Caprice would live to take Isabella's place and fulfill her role and destiny as the Council Queen. I wouldn't accept any other outcome.

8

CAPRICE

Academy Obscura was a walled fortress about twenty miles east of Estacada. Buried deep in the forest, I didn't see any sign of it until we were at the tall iron gates. They were open and we drove right through.

Inside was a complex of grey stone buildings. Isabella followed the driveway to the central building, which had turrets. It resembled a small castle. A few other cars were parked in the circular drive, letting out awestruck students. At least I wasn't the only one overwhelmed by this place.

Academy Obscura was carved into the stone, in an arch over the doorway. We walked through the heavy wooden doors, our shoes clopping on the polished stone floor. The late afternoon sunlight glowed in the leaded glass windows.

"You went to school here?" I asked Isabella. I still had a hard time wrapping my head around her actual age.

"Over a century ago." She glanced around the high-ceiling room. "It hasn't changed."

Against the far wall was a row of tables. The people behind them checked in students in, giving them their room assignments and class schedules. We joined the line.

"All I need to do is pass this year and those creeps will leave me alone?" I kept my voice low. This place made my skin crawl, but I wasn't sure why.

"That's correct," Isabella said. "You must try your best. This academy is highly competitive." She frowned, shifting her weight nervously even though she wasn't the one enrolling here today.

I didn't understand the connection between the school and the cannibals. When I asked Isabella questions about it, she just said that it was all part of the Truce's terms. So, I had to be a good student and I wouldn't get eaten. Not cool at all. Deranged, actually. Who thought up this arrangement?

I'd do anything to pass my classes. As long as I wasn't expected to do some witchy stuff, because I couldn't do any of that stuff. At least, not that I knew of.

The girl in front of us gave me a top to bottom once-over, sneered, then faced forward. Wow, not friendly. I doubted I'd make any friends, these people were all freaks after all, which made me miss Elena even more.

Soon it was our turn to approach the tables. A dark haired woman with an easy smile welcomed me.

"Caprice Sorrentino. Witch," she said. "You'll be in the witches' dorm. Last building on the left side. Room 219. Here's your key. All other materials are in your packet." She handed me the bulging manila envelope. "Orientation is at midnight tonight. Again details are in your packet."

"Uh, okay..."

Isabella tugged on my arm. "Let's go find your room and get you settled."

"Why is orientation at midnight?"

"Most academy business, and all classes, take place at night." She saw my confused expression. "It's easier that way. Witches, werewolves, shifters, and fae may be able to stand the daylight, but vampires certainly cannot."

I halted on the front steps. "Wait. I'm going to school with vampires? Like blood-sucking vampires?"

"I thought I'd told you all of that." Isabella brushed silver hair out of her face. "Sorry. Yes, vampires do drink blood but they don't drink from people. It's not like the movies—at least not any more. Don't worry about it."

"Don't worry about it? Are you insane? I was attacked by a vampire."

"I understand your concern. But you were attacked by a Tromara vampire. That's completely different. Look, it's going to take some time for you to acclimate to all of this. I wish I'd had more time to prepare you." She brushed past me to the car, ending the conversation.

After a moment, I descended the stairs and got into the passenger seat. Isabella was acting weird and I couldn't figure out why.

I silently chewed the inside of my cheek as we drove the short distance to a three story rectangular building. Above the door were the words: McIver Dorm, established 1872.

I had my two suitcases and a box of personal items from my old bedroom in Baltimore. Isabella carried the box and I took the rest up to the second floor. My room had a single large window in the far wall, two twin beds, two dressers, desks, and closets. I assumed at some point I'd be getting a roommate.

I chose the bed closest to the door, rolling the cases over to it. Isabella set the box down. She turned to me, wrapping me in a bone-crunching hug.

"I'm sorry about all of this. I'd hoped to send you to Europe for college, far away from here," she said. "But now that the Tromara know about you, that's impossible." She gripped my arms, her intense gaze shone with unshed tears. "We'll make the best of it. Follow the rules. Focus on your studies. Just pass this year, then next year will be easier." Tears slid down her cheeks and she wiped at them. "And after that you'll be done. Then you can choose any four year college you want." Isabella hugged me again.

"Okay. I will." I frowned into her hair. "Are you all right?"

She sniffed. "I'm so sorry," she whispered before pulling away. "Text me when you can. I love you."

"Love you too," I said as she slipped out of the room, confused by her intense emotions and apology. What could she possibly be sorry for? She was doing everything in her power to fight for me.

I sighed, sinking down to the edge of the bed. This was it. My first day—or rather night—of college had begun.

To pass the time, I took a long nap. Getting used to sleeping during the day and taking classes at night was going to be a challenge. My alarm went off at eleven o'clock. I didn't want to miss Orientation.

From the envelope, I pulled out a campus map and my schedule. Orientation was held in Sorrentino Hall, which was about a ten minute walk from my dorm. It was weird seeing my last name in the school's literature. These people probably knew my family's history, they certainly knew more than I did. I felt exposed.

My classes for the first quarter were:

11:00pm - 11:55pm - History - Gi Hall Rm 106
12:15am - 1:10am - Magic 101 - Aeras Hall Rm 100
Break
2:00am - 2:55am - Potions - Gi Hall Rm 201
3:15am - 4:10am - Mythology - Gi Hall Rm 311
Dinner

That didn't sound too bad. Except, I had a feeling that Jaxon was going to be my History teacher. His statement about his flirting with me being a means to an end still stung. What an asshole.

I looked myself over in the full length mirror that hung from the door. Not too bad for being up in the middle of the night. I decided to add my leather jacket to the jeans and T-shirt. It made me feel stronger, ready to face freaking vampires and a building with my name on it.

Heading to Sorrentino Hall, I tried to blend in with the several hundred other students and teachers. Honestly, they looked disappointingly normal. I figured the vampires were the ones with paler skin, but I couldn't be sure.

Against the flow, right toward me, moved a familiar tall, tan form. Angel. He winked when he spotted me in the crowd. Which made my knees go weak.

"Hey, Caprice," he said as he brushed past. His caramel eyes alight with flirtation.

I wanted to be cool and say hey back to him, instead I stared until he disappeared from view.

Someone cleared their throat, bringing me back to my surroundings. Five girls stood in front of me. Their arms folded, and their stances vaguely threatening.

The one in front studied me, a sneer twisting her lips. "Keep your eyes to yourself. Angel is mine."

"Whatever," I muttered, continuing to the Hall. Mean girls were nothing new to me, and I could spot them in an instant. Better not to engage. Besides, she could have Angel. He was friends with Jaxon after all, which put him in the asshole category, by association if nothing else.

Sorrentino Hall held a monstrously huge room with a vaulted ceiling and row after row of benches that faced a stage. I sat in the back row on the end, warily watching everyone file in. Most seemed to sit with pre-established cliques.

A hush fell over the hall as a tall, pixie-haired woman took the stage. She was probably in her forties, dressed in a long black robe that tied at her slim waist. As she took her place behind the podium, translucent wings sprouted from her shoulders.

I gaped for several seconds. They were beautiful, if a little disturbing. Blue and yellow light undulated within the wings' fragile structure.

"Good morning," she said, "I am Sophia Wright, Dean of Academy Obscura. I welcome you all." Her strong voice echoed in the Hall. "This school serves two purposes: To keep the Truce, and to teach supernaturals how to control their gifts, so that you may interact with the human world without putting us in danger. After two years here, you'll have an Associates Degree that is transferable to any four-year college. However," her gaze briefly dropped, "the lowest ten percent of students will not receive their degree. But they will be honored and respected for eternity by the supernatural community."

Several people around me glanced knowingly at each other. Talk about a competitive school, and a great way to get everyone starting to size each other up. Stay out of the lowest ten percent. Got it.

"Points status for each student will begin being posted once the first term concludes. For now, you'll need to focus on your studies. In order to do that, we've found that a distraction free environment is best." Dean Wright motioned toward several people at the back of the room. They started down the aisles with baskets. "Please hand your phone to our faculty members. Phone calls are allowed on the weekends only. You will have to come to my office to retrieve your device."

Now that was total crap! I pulled my cell out of my pocket. How was I supposed to stay in touch with Elena, or Isabella, or social media, or the world? Glancing at it, I noticed the text across the top: No Signal.

The phone-collector had arrived, holding the basket out for my device. With a sigh, I reluctantly handed it to him. He slipped it into a plastic bag and wrote my name on a label.

"Where is the dean's office?" I asked him.

"Dean's Hall, second floor."

I sighed.

He moved on down the row.

Only calls on the weekend. Only if I could get cell reception. This was going to be like the Dark Ages.

After taking all our precious devices away, Dean Wright continued with Orientation. "As you are new to the Academy, we have but one rule...don't go outside the walls for any reason. Ever. The Academy is not responsible for student safety." She put her palms together in a prayer-like gesture. "I wish you the best of luck for your Culling Year."

As she walked off the stage, students rose and headed for the doors. I shuffled into the stream of bodies.

This was one weird school. *Not* responsible for student safety? *Culling* Year? What did that even mean? What happened to the students who didn't graduate?

Something was not right about this place. A cold, prickly sensation spread over my shoulders. I had the feeling that more than my academic standing was going to be at stake.

I opened my dorm room door to the sound of muttering inside. Poking my head in, I found my roommate unpacking. She had purple and black hair, a tall willowy build, and wore a floral romper.

She squeaked when she saw me. "Oh, hello. I'm Madison Swan." She extended a hand.

"Caprice Sorrentino," I said, shaking it.

"Oh! A Sorrentino. I'm so excited. So..." she said, "we're in the same dorm, you must be a witch too. I mean, of course you are. Duh." Her big brown eyes made me think of Bambi's girlfriend.

I shrugged. "That's what they keep saying. It must be true."

"You don't know for sure? How can you not? My family is generation after generation of witches. Your's is too, but you already know that."

"Actually, I grew up in the foster system."

"Oh." She gazed at the floor. "Sorry."

"It's okay." I sat on my twin bed across the room. "How do you know you're a witch, besides all of your family being witches?"

She sat down. "Well, I...came into my gift at twelve. It was actually terrifying." Her large eyes stared into mine. "One moment I was sleeping and the next I woke up floating in the air. I screamed and fell to the floor. Of course my sisters and brother laughed. They're all older than me, so they've been through it all. They called me Baby Maddy for a long time, too. But not anymore. Now I'm at the Academy." Her gaze lit up with excitement.

Chatty Maddy would have been a better name for her, but at least she was nice.

"Do you like, cast spells and stuff?" I asked.

She laughed. "Oh no. Witches can't do that until we get our wands at the Academy." Madison peeked at me through her lashes. "You really don't know anything about being a witch do you?"

I shook my head.

"Have you ever wished really hard for something and it happened?" she asked.

I was used to a life where wishes didn't come true. But, I wasn't going to tell her that, it sounded way to melodramatic. "Nope. Never had that happen."

"Not once? It happens to me all the time. Once, I stole Mama's pie because I was really hungry and it smelled so good. She came after me with her broom—that's how mad she was— and I was so scared. But by the time she found my hiding spot the pie had disappeared. Just vanished from my hands. Of course, Mama knew I'd taken it. She couldn't prove it though." Madison frowned. "The sad thing is, that pie never came back. I don't know where the disappearing things go. Do you?"

"Not a clue. Like I said, I've never had anything like that happen."

Madison chewed on her thumbnail. "Are you nervous about tomorrow? First day of school?"

"A little, yeah." I leaned forward. "What do you know about this Culling Year and the bottom ten percent not getting to graduate? That seems really strange to me. And harsh."

Her eyes grew so wide, I was afraid they'd pop out. "You don't know about the culling?" She gasped. "Everyone knows about it."

"Well, I don't. Want to enlighten me?"

In a near whisper, she said, "The culling keeps the Truce alive."

When she didn't continue, I folded my arms. "I don't even know what that means." Why had Isabella sent me here in such a state of ignorance? Jaxon hadn't said a thing about any of this either. I felt like an idiot and a complete outsider.

"I'll tell you." She visibly swallowed. "The Tromara and the rest of the supernaturals used to fight a lot. But the Tromara were too strong—"

"I do know about the Tromara. Cannibals...and all that."

"Oh good. So they were too strong and the supernaturals were losing. They met and came up with the Truce. The terms they settled on are better than the alternative, even if is doesn't seem like it for us."

"And the Truce terms are..?"

"Basically a yearly sacrifice. Academy Obscura was created to make the sacrifice into an organized system. Every year the lowest ten percent of students are sacrificed to the Tromara."

I stared at her, brow furrowed. "You're not joking."

"No. I'd never joke about something like that. Freshman year here is a competition like no other. If you fall below the ten percent line... unknown horror awaits you at the end of the year. No one really knows what the Tromara do with their sacrifices, besides the obvious. Eat them." Madison wrapped her arms around her shoulders and shivered. "I come from a long line of witches, but there are no guarantees here."

Sweet Grandma Isabella had sent me to a school where I had to academically compete for my life. I wanted to cry and scream at the same time. Then a thought occurred to me. "Madison, are there other schools like this? In other parts of the world?"

"This Academy is the only one in the United States. Under the terms of the Truce, all supernaturals living in the country have to send their children here. For a while they were sending them overseas. When the Tromara found out they killed those entire families." Her forehead bunched. "No one does that anymore."

"My grandma had no choice then. As soon as the Tromara found out about me, she had to send me here." I said it to myself more than to her. But Isabella had talked about sending me to Europe for college. She was willing to risk her life to spare me having to go here. And I'd been stupid, going outside on the full moon. If only I'd listened to Isabella. If only I'd taken her seriously.

Again, I wanted to scream and cry. This was all my fault.

9

CAPRICE

At ten fifty-five the next night, I walked into my first class. Jaxon stood at the front of the room, ignoring the students as they filtered into History class. I immediately bristled, even though I'd been mentally preparing myself for having to face him today.

I slumped down in the back row. The further from him the better. He wore black slacks and white dress shirt that clung to his broad shoulders. I glanced away before he felt my gaze. That was when I noticed the front row was filled with those mean girls, their attention locked on him.

Whatever. They could have the jerk for all I cared.

A loud thump next to me drew my attention. Across the aisle sat a girl dressed in all black with long blond hair and heavy dark eyeliner. She curled her lips back when she caught me staring, showing off a pair of deadly fangs.

Holy fuck! She was a vampire. Averting my gaze, I rummaged in my backpack, pulling out a notebook and pen. I nervously tapped the end of the writing utensil on the wooden desk. Jaxon looked up from the papers he'd been shuffling. His gaze swept across the classroom's auditorium style seating. When he found me, his grey eyes hardened and his jaw worked. A moment later he was back to studying the top of his desk.

I sighed. This class was probably mandatory for first year students, otherwise he would have found a way out of being my teacher. Instead we both just had to make the best of it. And I had to make the best of sitting across from a vampire.

Someone snickered at the front of the room. The bitchy girls from yesterday sat in a cluster, and they were all staring at me. One of them glanced from Jaxon to me and back again, then whispered to the others. They giggled.

Great. Mean girls and Jaxon first thing in the morning. This was going to be a fantastic term. I groaned, trying to ignore the girls.

"Welcome to History 101. I'm Mr. McIver." Jaxon's voice rang strong and resonate in the stone-walled classroom. It sent tingles through me. I clenched my teeth against my body's reaction. "In this class, you'll learn all about the history of the supernatural and the Tromara. Please step forward to collect your textbook."

I was near the back of the line that shuffled toward Jaxon—or Mr. McIver. When my turn was up, I snagged the book from his desk. His gaze read over a paper in his hand, but his attention was on me. I could feel his commanding presence reaching out for me, once again threatening to engulf me.

For a second, it felt like this cold distance between us was all wrong. I wanted to reach out to him. Then I remembered that he was the one who'd created the distance, and his exact words. He'd been very clear about how much I did *not* mean to him. I retreated back to my seat in a hurry, accidentally bumping into the vampire.

"I'm so sorry," I said in a hushed tone.

She glared in response.

For the next forty minutes Jaxon lectured on the wars between the supernaturals and the Tromara, apparently there had been several wars fought before the one that led to the Truce.

"With the Truce came the Supernatural Council, whose job it is to uphold the terms of the Truce. The Council Queen's role is to oversee the other members, and she holds the ultimate authority in all decisions..." Jaxon continued.

I chewed on the pen cap. Council Queen? I didn't remember seeing her in the church with the rest of the members. If Jaxon wasn't the teacher for this class, I would have raised my hand and asked about her. But there was no way I was drawing attention to myself like that. Not from him.

"Since the Truce, there have been several rebellions." Jaxon's eyes took on a distant look, like he was remembering a specific incident. "They have all ended with the Tromara overpowering us. Each time they could have annihilated us all, but they didn't. It is by their mercy that we live. After the last rebellion, we were warned, that if another one followed they would enslave us all."

Jesus. These people must live in constant fear.

The bell rang, and it was on to Magic 101. Which had my gut all knotted up. I left the Gi Hall to walk next door to the Aeras Hall. Even though it was midnight, the campus was well lit with closely placed lamp posts. The four classroom buildings formed a square around the open lawn in the middle. The outer perimeter, where the dorms were, was thick with towering pines and cedars.

The Magic 101 classroom was a long, open space with benches down one side. Against the far wall were floor to ceiling cabinets with wooden doors and locks.

I sat just inside the door, at the end of a bench. Since no one else had come in yet, I snapped my fingers, willing them to spark, or flame, or anything.

"What are you doing?"

I glanced up into Madison's round eyes. "Nothing. Just trying to get a flame to light."

"Oh, you mean like this?" She snapped her fingers and a perfect orange and yellow light danced to life.

I sighed, crossing my arms over my chest. "Exactly like that."

"Don't worry, you'll get the hang of it." Madison sat next to me. "I'm so excited, aren't you?"

"For what?"

She gave me a startled glance. "This is where we get our wands. I've been dreaming about this day for years. I wonder which one will call to me. And which one will call to you. They're all unique, no one will ever have a wand like either of ours."

Great. I felt like no magic ran in my blood, and I was supposed to have a wand call to me.

The room quickly filled with students. A couple seconds before class started, the teacher arrived. She was a short, round woman with deep lines on her face and electric blue hair.

"Oh, my students," her voice boomed, "how wonderful. Look at you all. I know this day has been a fantasy for all of you for so long. Now it is finally here." She paused for dramatic effect. "Today, you become true witches. Today, you take the power of wielding magic into your own hands. Today, is your day."

I regarded her with a slightly cocked head. Cray-cray. The Shake-spearian troop left town without their lead witch from Macbeth.

"As I call you forward, please step up to receive your wand." She walked to the far wall, pulling a long blue object from her flowy dress pocket. With a swish and a muttered word, the cabinet doors unlocked to reveal a wall of wands.

Each hung horizontally on the wall from a two small brackets. Although long and tapered, they weren't made of wood, as I'd expected. Instead they came in all colors, some had multiple colors, veins, or flecks. They were made from a variety of crystals and stones.

"Now," said the teacher, "I'm Ms. Duinn. And I'm going to start at the top of the alphabet." A long scroll unrolled in her hand. "Mr. Aimes."

A boy with short reddish-brown hair stood up from the bench. He must have been related to the councilor Aimes. Probably his son.

Ms. Duinn waved him forward. "Young man, you must stand here in the middle, facing the wall of wands. Now close your eyes and reach out your hand. Let your wand call to you. Don't fret, just let it happen. Good, good."

A hush fell over the benches. Aimes stood silently for several long seconds. His feet shuffled to the left, then forward until he almost bumped into the wall. Several feet above his head, a clear wand with black flecks began to glow. As the glowing intensified, it wiggled out of its brackets, plummeting toward the boy. He caught it.

Turning to face us, he held the wand high. His pale green eyes lit with victory. Everyone around me cheered and clapped. Getting your wand was a big deal. Even Madison beamed, squirming excitedly in her seat.

It took a while to get to the S section of the alphabet. I was up first with Sorrentino, next would be Madison Swan. By the time Ms. Duinn called out my name, I was nervous as all hell.

"Sorrentino?" someone whispered the question. "Where'd she come from?"

I rose, wiping the sweat from my palms onto my jeans. Going to stand in the middle of the room, I followed the protocol. Eyes closed, hand reaching toward the wall of wands. Besides that, I didn't know what else to do.

I stood there for what seemed like forever, but it was probably about thirty seconds. A couple of people started murmuring behind me, as my face grew warm from embarrassment. I didn't feel anything. No urge to walk forward. Nothing.

Peeking through my lashes up at the wall, not one wand glowed. This was useless. I lowered my hand.

"Have no fear," Ms. Duinn said. "This happens sometimes." She leaned close to my ear. "Stay a while after class."

I nodded, going to retake my seat.

"Don't worry, Caprice," Madison said, "you'll get one too. I know you will.

She was up next. Of course, immediately a purple crystal wand glowed and took flight from the wall.

She returned to the bench, her doe eyes wide as she studied her wand. "Isn't this amazing? Look at all the little white veins in the amethyst."

I admired her wand. It was pretty.

Once class was dismissed, and everyone had their wands except me, I approached Ms. Duinn.

She took me by the arm. "You need to relax to hear the call. Come. Stand here, close your eyes, and reach out."

I did as she said. With deep breaths in, I tried to relax and let something—anything—happen. Nothing did. I felt nothing just like before.

Ms. Duinn clucked her tongue. "Open your eyes, Ms. Sorrentino. Let's go with this one." She waved her own wand at the wall, dislodging a piece made from obsidian. It didn't glow as it floated toward me, instead it was a shiny black.

I reached out, and plucked it in mid-air. "But it didn't call to me."

"No worries. The connection between witch and wand is strongest when it is naturally formed, but any wand will do. I think this one suites you fine. After a time you may even bond with it." She smiled, showing small white teeth. "Now off to lunch with you."

I grabbed my backpack with my free hand, and left the hall. Outside, under a light post, I studied the obsidian wand. It was uniform in color, so shiny that it reflected like a tiny mirror along its roughly eight inch length.

"Did that one glow for you or whatever?" Angel asked, coming up to stand next to me. He wore slacks and a black button-down shirt with the sleeves rolled up. I wondered which subject he taught, imagining the students in the front row of his class eating up the sight of him.

My breath hitched as his dark gaze met mine. Regaining my composure, I asked, "Or whatever? You're not a witch are you?"

One side of his mouth lifted in a smirk. "No."

When he didn't say more, I hesitated. "Uh, do I even want to ask?"

"I don't know, do you?" He shoved his hands in his pockets, moving closer. "Are you curious?" His breath rustled my hair. A shiver ran down my neck. But my eyes never left his for a moment.

I sucked in a breath. "I am curious." My voice came out in a whisper.

His gaze darted to my lips. He growled low. It was an animal sound, no human could make that noise.

I took a step back, my heart beating against my ribcage. Oh my God, I knew what he was, what he had to be. I didn't want to believe it. Swallowing hard, I said, "You're a werewolf. Aren't you?"

His amber eyes had taken on a golden glow, turning them almost yellow. Without a word, he turned, and hurried away, shoulders taut and hunched.

I stared at his back. What had just happened there?

Potions class was an herb soup disaster. I'd measured out everything, followed the instructions in the textbook, but my stupid wand wouldn't work no matter what I tried.

"Miss Sorrentino, you need to channel your inner magic through your wand. It won't do anything on its own," May said. Besides being absolutely gorgeous, she was also kind, giving me most of her attention during class. Her strawberry hair hung down her back, growing frizzy in the humid air of surrounding bubbling cauldrons.

"I don't think I have any magic in me," I muttered, pointing my wand at the big black pot again. I was holding a rock. A cold, black rock that was completely useless in this magical world.

"You need to take some time to unlock your abilities," May said. With a sympathetic smile she finally gave up on me, moving on to evaluate the next student.

I left class feeling absolutely defeated, slowly making my way down the rapidly emptying hallway. Maybe I was a dud. Were dud witches a thing?

A large body slammed against my shoulder, pushing me into another large person.

"Hey!" I said, trying to keep my balance.

Three guys blocked the hall in front of me, arms crossed over their chests. I recognized Aimes from Magic class. The other two sat with him in there and in Potions. One was tall and blond, the other beefy with brown hair and eyes.

"Sorrentino," Aimes said. "You're a real loser aren't you? Can't summon a wand. Can't brew a basic potion. You're a disgrace to your family name."

I didn't have to stand there and listen to him. I moved to push past the three big brutes. Mean boys, just like mean girls, were best left alone and ignored.

Aimes caught my arm, digging his fingers into my flesh. "I can't wait to see you get culled." His buddies laughed, the tall blond one clapping him on the back. Aimes shoved me away. "See you around Sorrentino."

I rubbed my sore arm, sure there would be a bruise. My eyes stung, watching them joke with each other as they rounded the corner. I'd never done anything to them. Why were they being so mean to me?

Flashes of old memories came to me. Each new school brought a new group of bullies, whether they were guys or girls. The lonely, sad foster kid was an easy mark. Most of the time I just ignored them, not letting their insults get to me. At least that's what I'd told myself. That I didn't care. But every word they spoke had cut me deep and left a scar.

I sniffed, wiping the tears from my cheeks. I wasn't the outcast anymore. I had a family now. Now, I belonged somewhere and with someone. Which made what Aimes said hurt even more. Was I a disgrace to the Sorrentino family name? I had a sinking feeling that I was.

I straightened my spine, walking with purpose toward my next class on third floor of Gi Hall. I couldn't let them get to me or I'd never survive.

The bell rang, and I sprinted up the stairs to Mythology. Damn, I was late. And on the first day, too. Wrenching open the door, I peered inside. Then paused as my gaze locked with Jaxon's other friend, Liam.

The class turned to glance at me. Horrified, I quickly sat down just inside the door.

"Nice of you to join us, Miss Sorrentino," Liam said. "Normally tardiness is a five point deduction. Since it's the first day of classes, I will let it slide."

I nodded. "Thank you, sir."

"Now where was I...ah, yes. In this class you'll learn what is real and what is myth." Liam paced the front of the classroom, making eye contact with the students. His tousled red hair fell into kind green eyes.

I slouched in my seat, this disastrous day replaying in my mind. The more I thought about it, the more a sense of doom crowded into my consciousness. If I didn't get it together and find my magic soon, I was going to be handed over to the Tromara at the culling. I shuddered.

The culling seemed like a vague concept rather than reality. These people didn't really sacrifice their kids to a bunch of supernatural cannibals. Did they? It seemed impossible. My brain refused to grasp this idea.

Liam's lecture returned to my awareness. "...and the like. Then there are some that are debated to this day. For example, dragons or dragon-shifters. Some say they are myth, while others disagree..."

How could I find my magic? I should have asked Isabella more questions about witches. I could talk to her on the weekends, but that was it. She was limited to telling me things, she couldn't show me how to do anything.

If the situation was different, I'd turn to Jaxon for help. But...that wasn't likely to happen. Besides, why would he help me? I was practically a stranger to him and the rest of these people. They had no reason to care whether I lived or died. Only Isabella cared. I was sure of that.

"Miss Sorrentino?" Liam asked.

I startled. How long had he been calling my name? My face heated, but I sat up straighter. "Yes, sir? Sorry."

"I need you to stay after class." Liam pursed his lips, then went back to lecturing.

I buried my face in my hands. Now I was in trouble. Great. This day could not get any worse.

10

CAPRICE

The class emptied out. My stomach twisted up so tight, I thought I was going to be sick.

Once the last person had left, Liam strode up the aisle and closed the door.

I frowned up at him. "What are you—?"

"Don't worry, Caprice, I just want to speak with you." He sat down on my desk. His gentle moss-colored eyes held concern. "You've had a rough day."

I opened my mouth, then closed it when nothing came out. I tried again. "How do you know that?"

"I'm a fae. We have empathic abilities." He folded his hands in his lap. "I can feel all of the fear, worry, anger, and sadness that you're feeling right now."

I ducked my head. I didn't want anyone to know how I felt, it was embarrassing.

"Do you want to tell me what happened today?" Liam asked. "Did something in particular upset you?"

If he thought I was going to open up to him, he was way wrong. I shook my head. "Just first day at a new school kinds of things. I'll be fine."

Liam sat quietly for a long moment. "As your teacher, I care about how you're doing with your classes. I want you to know that I'm here for you, whenever you need to talk to someone."

I gave him a dubious look. "Right. Thanks." I didn't know him. Or trust him. Plus he was Jaxon's friend.

He stood up, going to open the door. I followed, darting out of the room as soon as he unblocked the way. What a creep.

The dining hall, which was on the second floor of Sorrentino Hall, showed how cliquish this school was. Madison caught my arm as soon as I finished going through the dinner line. Dinner at five in the morning would take some getting used to.

"You'll want to sit over here," she said, steering us toward a table in the corner. As we passed the other tables, she murmured, "vampire table, werewolves, shifters, second years…us."

We scooted in at one end. The table was filled with other witches that I recognized from both Magic and Potions. Though, luckily, Aimes and his crew were not among them. They sat two tables over with a bunch of other witches.

"What's up with the two witch tables?" I asked Madison, while digging into the mashed potatoes.

"Oh gosh, you really don't know anything." Her round eyes searched my face. "There are two witch cliques, and you'd better be in one of them. This table is for the Italian clique, that other one is for the UK. Aimes, MacTavish, and Bennett lead the United Kingdom witches circle." She made a sour face. "Watch out for them, they're not nice people."

I was already well aware of that. "And who leads the Italian circle?"

"Traditionally, the Sorrentinos."

I choked on my potatoes. "What?"

"I know you only just came out of the foster system, but I would've thought your grandma would have told you all of this. Even my family knows about it and we're rather ordinary in the witch community." Madison sighed. "But since you don't know, and no one else seems to be telling you anything...I guess I will."

"What are you talking about?"

"The Sorrentino family is a big deal because they're—you're—the royal line. Right now your grandma is the queen, and you'll take her place some day. If you survive this year, of course, which I hope you do."

My mouth hung open. Isabella was the queen? When she said she wanted me to be her heir, she didn't just mean the house and her wealth. She meant heir to the Council position that she held, too. Why hadn't she told me?

I let my fork fall onto the tray. This whole day was too much to take. Suddenly, I felt exhausted, and no longer hungry. "Is there anything else I should know?" I asked.

"Probably lots." Madison stabbed at her salad. "We can do a kind of a current events 101 together over the weekend if you want to. Mama is always up on the latest events and gossip and everything like that, so I know more than most people about the Council and their families."

"Yeah, that would be great. Thanks, Madison." My brows pulled together. "Your last name's Swan, isn't that English? Why aren't you part of the UK witches?"

Madison waved a dismissive hand. "Like I said, my family is a bit weird. Our ancestors sided with the Italians, and now the UK circle calls us traitors. But it's okay, because I like this side much better. I mean, have you met Aimes?"

"Unfortunately."

"Well, watch out for everyone at that table. They've been plotting to get the Council crown since the beginning. To take it from the Italians. Aimes' dad is in the only elected position, so they're really trying to maneuver their family into a better long-term position. At least that's what Mama says."

I glanced over at the other table. Aimes was obviously the leader, he held everyone's attention captive. When he finished speaking, they all laughed. One of his cronies, either MacTavish or Bennett, noticed me watching them. He elbowed Aimes in the side to get his attention.

Aimes turned toward me with a sneer twisting his lips. "Like what you see, Sorrentino?" he called out. "Come here and sit on my lap." Everyone at his table snickered.

I turned away. "Ew! What a creep." Standing up with my tray in hand, I said to Madison, "I'm going back to the room."

After depositing the tray in the bin, I headed across campus to my room. This night could go to hell and burn.

Unfortunately, the first night of school only set the tone for the rest of the week. On Friday we got our first test scores. I was passing History and Mythology, but failing Magic and Potions. No big surprises there.

When I arrived at my room after dinner that night, a note was posted on the door:

Attn: Sorrentino. Meet your advisor in staff office 09 immediately.

As soon as I finished reading it, it vanished in a sparkling blue fire. Magic notes. I should have guessed.

The staff offices were diagonally across campus from my dorm. I cut across the lawn for a more direct route. The early morning dew glistened in the lamplight, soaking into the fabric of my tennis shoes.

I didn't even know I had an advisor, much less who it was. A witch most likely.

This building was just called Academy Hall. Like the others it was made of stone blocks and had three floors. Knocking on the door to office number 09, I waited several seconds for a response. The hallway was empty and quiet. It was a couple of hours before dawn, and most people were still at dinner.

The door swung open. I came face to face with Jaxon. A groan escaped my throat before I could stop it.

Jaxon lifted a brow. He stepped to the side, waving me in.

I hesitated on the threshold. His words in the magic shop, and the week he'd spent ignoring me in his classroom, sent a rush of anger through me. He thought he could summon me whenever he wanted. Jerk me around as he liked.

I folded my arms over my chest, still standing in the doorway. "What do you want?"

"Get in here. Now." His voice as steely as his eyes.

"No." I lifted my chin. He wasn't the boss of me.

Jaxon grabbed my upper arm, dragging me into his office, as he slammed the door shut. He stood with his back to it, giving me no escape. Then he hauled me closer so that we were face to face. "May says you're failing Potions."

"Get your hands off me." I returned his glare.

He released me, folding his arms to mirror my stance. "What's going on, Caprice? Why are you failing?"

"Because I'm not a witch!" I yelled up at him. I wasn't going to let him intimidate me or jerk me around any more.

"The hell you're not!" He raked a hand through his blond hair. "Do you know what happens if you fail?"

Now he wanted to talk about this, to clue me in? Anger boiled in my chest. I took a deep breath, biting down on my lip to gain control of myself. "Yes, I know. No thanks to you. You and Isabella kept me in the dark to get me here. So you could enroll me in this savage school." I poked him in his hard abs. "You're a manipulative asshole!"

"And you're a defiant little bitch!" His jaw muscles worked. "You know you're a witch, I know you're a witch. What are you playing at by failing? This is not a game—"

"I'm not going to stand here while you insult me and call me names."

"You started it," he growled.

"What are you, a child? I have nothing to say to you. Get out of my way."

He shook his head. "Why are you failing?"

"I already told you." I clenched my teeth. "I can't do magic."

"That's impossible. You're being lazy or not trying hard enough." He leaned toward me. "I won't let you fail this year. I won't let you be culled. Now you either try harder on your own, or I'll figure out a way to motivate you."

I swallowed hard. Now the asshole was threatening me? "You don't listen, do you?" I moved to his side, trying to shove him away from the door. Since I was about half his size, it wasn't very effective.

He glared down at me, not budging an inch. "You're not leaving here until you explain yourself."

"I already have! You're not listening." I shoved at him again, inhaling his unique scent of oatmeal soap and spice. The warmth of his body seeped through my clothes.

He widened his stance to further cement himself in place.

"You can't keep me here like this," I said. "You're a teacher, there are rules...laws against this sort of thing."

His laugh was short and unamused. "This is Academy Obscura. The only rules here are don't go beyond the walls, and try not to get culled." He pushed off from the door. "I can do anything I want to you."

I turned the knob and bolted into the hallway. My heart beating so fast and hard, it was all I could hear as I sprinted back to my dorm.

Madison ended up not having time that weekend to fill me in on supernatural current events. She'd gotten a lower score than she wanted in Potions, so she spent all weekend studying. I decided to do the same. I had to get this wand to work, or there'd be no hope for me. But first, I had a phone call or two to make.

I trudged down the well-lit pathway to the administration building in search of Dean Wright. She was in her office on the second floor, a long line of students trailed down the hallway waiting to get their cell phones from her. I joined the end of the line. Luckily, they had an efficient system in place and in ten minutes I'd passed through the receptionists outer office and into the dean's.

The room was brightly lit, reflecting off the huge glass desk near the far wall. Dean Wright sat behind it with her assistants handing out cell phones.

My phone was still in its labeled plastic bag. I had to sign for it before she'd give it to me.

"There should be reception in either of the turrets." Dean Wright waved me off. "Next!"

I followed several other students down the hall, then up a winding flight of stairs that opened into a circular room. Turning the cell on, the screen brightened, showing three bars. I tapped the buttons to call Isabella.

"Caprice, it's so good to hear from you. How are you?" It was one in the morning but she sounded wide awake.

A flurry of emotions whirled in me. I was happy to hear her voice. I wanted to scream at her for dropping me off in this hellhole. And I had so, so many questions.

I drew in a deep breath. "Why didn't you tell me what this place was?"

"I'm so sorry. I couldn't." She sighed. "I was afraid that you'd run if I told you everything. The Tromara would have hunted you down, but they also would have killed me, and there would be far-reaching consequences to that for the supernatural community—"

"I know you're the Council Queen. Why didn't you tell me that?" I leaned against the cool stone wall, trying not to be overheard by everyone else in the room.

"I wanted to tell you. Again, I was afraid that it would overwhelm you. That you'd feel burdened by this potential responsibility. I'm sorry," she said again.

"Right. Instead I show up here where there's a building with my name on it. Everyone knows who I am except for me." I let out a frustrated grunt. "I'm flying blind here!"

"I know. I'm sorry—"

"Stop saying that!"

A long moment of silence followed.

"I was wrong, Caprice. I know that now. I had a decision to make about how to handle this and I made the wrong one. Let me try to make it right. Ask me anything."

"What happens to those who are culled?" I asked over the din in the echoey room. "Is that even for real?"

"It is. The Truce is designed to remind us of who we owe our lives to. The Tromara let the majority of us live as long as we don't break any of the rules and make the yearly sacrifice. I don't know exactly what the Tromara do with the culled. No one does."

"You really let them do this? You're the leader. Can't you stop this?"

"No. You don't know how bad it was before the Truce. As hard as it is, sacrificing twenty or so of our young people is worth the heartache." She didn't sound convinced of her own words.

Nothing she said would make me understand this. "Okay, what else do I need to know about this place, or myself, or our family?"

"Well, we are the ruling royal family. Before I found you, and with your father gone, I was worried about the crown. About who it would go to next. Even though there is a line of succession, I knew there would be fighting, maybe even war if a Sorrentino wasn't there to take the crown. I need you to survive—because I love you, and because you need to rule after I'm gone."

She continued, "I've made Jaxon promise to help you and keep you safe."

"What?" I said it too loud, getting annoyed glances from those closest to me. "Are you crazy? He doesn't even like me."

"Regardless of his feelings toward you, he's there to help. Let him."

I groaned.

"Try, Caprice. You're on your own without him. I can't even begin to convey how dangerous a position that puts you in. The Tromara and the culling are the least of your worries right now. The politics, power-plays, and long-held grudges are what you need to watch out for. Many of your classmates are related to the other ruling families and others have chosen which side they're loyal to. If you don't have any allies, they'll tear you apart."

I gulped. This place really was a hellhole. "I don't have any experience with this kind of stuff. What will they try to do to me?"

"I don't know. Just be on your guard. Make friends where you can, but be careful. Trust Jaxon to guide you. Okay?"

"All right." I looked around at my fellow classmates on their phones. Which of them was out to get me? Which held a grudge against my family name? I was so out of my depths.

"I have to get to a meeting. Call me next weekend?" Isabella asked.

"I will. Bye."

For several seconds I stared at the blank screen. I thought my life had gotten so much better now that I'd found my family. Instead it had become complicated beyond my wildest imaginings. I was supernatural royalty. Shit.

With a few thumb strokes, I sent a text to Antonio telling him that I was fine and settling into my new school. And that I missed all of them.

A million text messages had piled up from Elena. Instead of sifting through them, I called her. But it was really late back east and the call went to voicemail. I hung up, texting her back instead.

So, this school sucks and we don't have cell coverage except on weekends. I'm doing okay. Jaxon is one of my teachers this term, blah. How are your classes? Any hot guys? Fun parties? I hope you're being careful.

After sending the text, I reluctantly turned my phone to the dean. Tomorrow I'd get it back and respond to whatever Elena wrote. There was so much I wanted to tell her that I couldn't. It was driving me crazy. I pushed my frustration aside. Right now, I needed to find a place to get in touch with my magic.

I decided to wander the forest behind my dorm, it seemed secluded. The last thing I wanted was for someone to stumble upon me while I was trying to get a handle on my wand. Failing in class was embarrassing enough.

I walked deeper into the spice-scented evergreens. Instead of thinking of magic, I tried to wrap my brain around Isabella and the queen role. My whole life, I'd thought I was a normal person. Unfortunate circumstances had placed me in the foster system, but when I got out, I had plans for a normal life. I craved stability and to blend in with everyone else for a change.

It seemed that fate had other plans.

Council Queen. Did I even want that responsibility? I wasn't sure. Hopefully, Isabella lived a long life. Another twenty or thirty years didn't seem unreasonable at her age. I snorted, she was already a hundred and fifty years old. But another decade or so might be enough time for me to figure out who I was and what I was doing with my life.

I chewed on the inside of my cheek. If I made it through this year at Academy Obscura, of course. Which was not a given. Especially surrounded by my grandma's political enemies.

And what was Jaxon's problem? As my advisor, I figured he was supposed to *help* me. Isabella had made him promise. That interaction in his office had not been helpful at all. A shiver ran through me. I wished I could stop being attracted to him.

The woods pressed in around me, making me feel isolated yet safe. Away from all the people, and all the problems that came with them. I inhaled deeply to center myself. My grandmother was a witch, my father had been a witch, and I was a witch. Magic had to be in me *somewhere*.

Ms. Duinn said that magic casting came from concentration and intent. There were no words to cast spells, only intention that was focused through the stone wand. Or, in the case of more advanced and powerful witches, through their hands. Like when Jaxon produced flames with his fingers.

I shook my head. Any thought about Jaxon was a distraction.

Inhaling again, I took out my wand. I needed to try something easy. Glowing. I'd start with that.

The obsidian in my hand was shiny and dark. I held it firmly but with a relaxed grip, thinking about making the wand glow. I stared at it, focusing my intention.

After a moment my hand started to feel warmer, but that was all. The wand remained stubbornly dark.

I pushed harder, closing my eyes to shut out the world. My hand grew warmer still. Sweat made my grip slippery. This had to be working.

I glanced at the obsidian. Not glowing. Then I looked at my hand, and shrieked, dropping the wand into the fern at my feet.

My skin was covered in black scales. I turned my hand over, watching in horror as the scales glowed with a reddish hue, as if coals burned under them.

What the hell was going on? This was all wrong.

A chill swept over my scalp, and I shivered. In the next moment, the scales started to fade from my hand, until it was back to normal. I pinched the skin on my fingers. No trace of the black scaly texture was left.

I stared at my hand for many jolting heartbeats. Was I infected with some kind of disease? Had the magic I was trying to pour into the wand backfired? I rubbed my now cool-temperatured extremity as terror clawed at my chest. What was happening to me?

11

ANGEL

For some reason we always hung out in Jaxon's campus apartment during the school year. When the three of us were growing up together, Jaxon's house had been our base camp. I guessed old habits didn't die.

The campus rooms were okay. They all had a sitting room, kitchen, and a separate bedroom, like a real apartment. Liam and I sat on a sofa, watching Jaxon pace and rant.

"She's so goddamn stubborn!" Jaxon was saying. "Do you think she's failing because she really can't do magic? That's impossible. She has power in her, I can feel it. That damn Tromara vampire felt it too..."

Normally, I'd tell him to chill the fuck out. But I was feeling much edgier these past couple of weeks too. I'd been able to avoid Caprice, although I wasn't sure how much that was easing the panic that crept up in my gut several times a day.

I'd meant to use my charm, something both Jaxon and Liam lacked, to get closer to Caprice. Protecting someone was easier if you were friends with them. She was easy on the eyes too, which had me looking forward to spending some time around her.

Then I'd come across her that first night of classes, and I had flirted because that was what I always did. I was good at it. I'd gotten close to her, inhaled that floral scent of her hair, and my wolf had stirred. *Mate.* The word, more of a feeling, had flooded my chest.

My wolf had wanted to take her, right there under that lamp post. I'd *growled* at her, for God's sake! Thankfully, I was able to control myself enough to walk away, even though my cock had been so hard I thought I was going to burst.

Even thinking about it made me adjust my seat on the couch.

Liam said, "You're not helping any of us, Jaxon. Back off with her. She's not the type to be bullied into anything. Let me try my approach. I know it will work better."

"What's your approach? The soft one?" Jaxon asked. "Why don't you try some of that mind control on her and compel her to get her shit together."

Liam bristled next to me. "I won't use compulsion…"

Half of my mind tracked their conversation, I'd heard this same argument before. Jaxon argued that his way was best, while Liam countered with other ideas. They never came to a resolution.

Mate. My shoulders tensed. I'd slept with lots of women. I enjoyed it and so did they. Not once had my wolf had an opinion on any of them. This couldn't be happening now, not with the Sorrentino girl.

That she was a student, didn't matter. Teachers and students had relations all the time at Academy Obscura. It was taboo in the human world, but here, when you could have only a few more months to live, it was common to make the most of that time. I'd had sex with my fair share of fellow students when I attended here, and then some pupils once I'd come back as a teacher. But *mating* was different.

All wolves knew that if they were lucky they'd find a mate at some point in their life. My dad had told me all about it, how it had happened with him and my mom. Once your inner wolf responds to someone, the next step is to bond. And of course, be chosen in return by that other person. I figured if I stayed clear of Caprice, then the bonding and her choosing me were unlikely to happen.

"Don't you have anything to say about this?" Jaxon stood in front of me, arms crossed, eyes narrowed.

I didn't need to have Liam's empathic skills to see what was going on with Jaxon. My wolf senses picked up on the smell of lust that mingled with Jaxon's annoyance and fear. He had it bad for the Sorrentino girl. He wanted her. And he was terrified of losing her.

My wolf wanted to rip his head off.

"I agree with Liam," I said, keeping my gaze locked on Jaxon's.

He took a step back, plopping into the other sofa across from us, and buried his face in his hands. "Fine. Go for it. She's driving me crazy, and I don't even know why."

Liam and I exchanged a knowing glance.

I stood. "I've got papers to grade." Jaxon waved a hand above his head, and Liam gave me a parting nod.

I jogged down the flight of stairs to the ground level and staff offices. Coming toward me was this year's werewolf girl pack. They were always the same. Cliquish, haughty, and trying to get into my bed. Not that they wanted me only for a fun romp. They were after my position and family name.

Right now my dad was the alpha of the Pacific Pack and sat on the Supernatural Council. Diego Cortez was a powerful and wealthy man. When he died, both of those positions, and his money, went to me.

"Hey, Mr. Cortez," said the wolf girls' ringleader. She batted her eyelashes up at me while thrusting out her chest.

I gave a curt nod, stepping past them and walking with determination to my office. I knew from experience that if I gave them even the slightest bit of encouragement, they'd latch on like a wolf with a rabbit. And I was the rabbit.

No, my mate had to be chosen carefully. She had to be from a good family, preferably with wealth and power of their own. She'd one day be a councilman's wife. It was important that she fit that role. And most importantly, she had to be a werewolf. The Cortez line went back thousands of years. We were wolves. We never chose a mate outside of our own supernatural kind. My father forbade it.

I had to keep my wolf in check. The Sorrentino girl was not an option for me. The sooner she fell into Jaxon's—or any other guy's arms, the better. My anguished growl echoed in the empty hallway.

12

CAPRICE

I'd agonized over my options, but finally decided on not telling anyone about the black scales. Instead, I went to the library and did my own research. There wasn't much to go on, but it could have been a random flare up of a skin disease actually called Black Scale. Though that usually needed treatment. More likely, it was the result of pent up magic trapped in my hand, which apparently did happen to some witches. In which case I was lucky to not have been left with the resulting burns.

I called Isabella every Saturday night. We chatted about my lack of progress, but there was nothing she could do about it. At least the other students were mostly leaving me alone, though I still watched my back at all times.

On Saturday and Sundays I also returned Elena's texts. Which were becoming more and more superficial, since I couldn't tell her about this insane supernatural world. So we texted about boys, hot teachers, and her fun times at UMBC parties. Which only rubbed in how much my school life sucked. And how I didn't have a social life.

I managed to slip in a quick text here and there to Antonio and Vanessa, too. The last thing I needed was Antonio getting suspicious and coming out here after me. Keeping up this everything-is-fine act was tiring.

The next couple of weeks went by without incident. Jaxon went back to ignoring me in History class, he never summoned me to his office again either.

This Friday's lecture was turning interesting. He spoke from the front of the room like a golden god and no one could look away. I swore he got more attractive each time I saw him. By the end of the term I was sure to go blind from his sheer radiance. But I never let myself forget what an asshole he was, so that helped.

"The Tromara are not like the rest of supernaturals," Jaxon said. "Most of us have lifespans about twice as long as humans. We're not immortal. But the Tromara are. They are the same supernaturals we've been dealing with since before the Truce."

The more I learned about the Tromara, the more interesting and creepy they became. Their leader was like three hundred years old. Very few people ever saw him, but those who did said that he didn't look old.

Jaxon continued. "When the Truce was made, and this school was built, the terms of the culling were established. But the Tromara never specified who would be culled. The Council decided it was best to sacrifice the weakest among us to the Truce. Thus the lowest ten percent was chosen."

He talked about it as if it were normal and accepted. After a hundred and fifty years, I supposed that people would grow used to all of this. But I couldn't. The whole situation struck me as barbaric.

The Tromara were bullies. They ruled with fear, and the entire supernatural community let them do it. More than let them. They sacrificed their children to them. Every. Single. Year.

It made me sick. I'd never be the queen, because I wouldn't be able to live with myself if I perpetuated this disgusting arrangement. How did Isabella do it year after year? She didn't strike me as unfeeling.

The goth vampire across the aisle was chewing noisily on the eraser end of a pencil. I'd sat in the same spot for weeks, but she still freaked me out. Even the haughty werewolf girls in the front row didn't mess with her.

On the way out of Gi Hall, I spotted Angel walking toward me. He glanced up, raked his gaze over my body, then abruptly made a ninety-degree turn. I could only assume that Jaxon had told him something awful about me.

"I guess I don't have to worry about you hooking up with my man," said Destiny, queen of the wolf-girl clique. She stood with her hands on her hips. Her pack was made up of the twins Jade and Amber, Emma, and Rachel.

"Whatever," I muttered, turning to leave.

Rachel stepped in front of me. "I heard you're a dud witch."

Destiny's laugh was annoyingly high pitched. She spread her arms wide. "Come on, cast a spell on me, Dud."

I shoved past them. They snickered as I walked away. Having all of the other witches know that I couldn't work magic was bad enough, if those five knew then everyone on campus would know soon. They would make sure of that.

In Magic we practiced summoning objects. Well, everyone else practiced while I stood in the lineup watching Madison bring first her backpack, then mine, floating toward us.

After class, I stayed to talk with Ms. Duinn.

"I'm failing," I said. "How can I stop failing?"

She flourished a hand in the air. "Find your magic. Let it out."

"Have you ever had a student like me before? A witch who couldn't...cast?"

"All witches can cast. Find it and let it out."

I sighed. "How? How do I find it?"

"Everyone is unique. You'll find your way." She spun away quickly, making the air billow her flowing skirt.

I was going to get eaten by cannibals because my magic teacher couldn't teach me how to use magic. With a clenched jaw, I grabbed my bag, determined to find my inner witch.

She certainly didn't come out in Potions class. I stood over a cold cauldron of wolfsbane and yarrow, waving my wand at it like an idiot as I recited the incantation for the sixth time.

May made her way around the room, peering into bubbling, steaming liquid. As she halted before my cauldron, she wore a frown that was reserved only for me.

"No luck?" she asked.

I shook my head.

"Go ahead and dump it out then." She moved to the next student, still wearing that worried, pitying expression.

I took the heavy iron pot to the sink, dumping the failed potion down the drain, while mentally kicking myself for being such a failure.

Mythology was my favorite class. No wolf-bitches, no witch-bullies, and no magic.

Liam always had a smile and a softly spoken greeting when I arrived. Today he was passing back our mid-week assignment on chimeras.

He set the paper on my desk. "Good work, Caprice."

I smiled up at him. I was getting used to the high marks in this class. If only I could do so well in all the others.

I filed the paper away in my completed assignments folder while casually watching Liam move about the room. The other students reacted to him the same way I did. Their faces brightened and relaxed. He exuded warmth, calmness, and safety. It was probably a fae thing, but I hadn't met too many other ones. So maybe it was a Liam thing.

Today's lecture was on the trials of Hercules. Liam's gentle but strong voice filled the room, and I found myself lost in its cadence.

All too soon, the bell rang to end class. Reluctantly, I left to grab dinner, then give this wand another shot.

I munched on a turkey sandwich as I trudged deeper into the woods. Dawn wouldn't come for several hours, so I had time to try to get this wand to work. Honestly, I felt like giving up. If my life weren't on the line, I would have given up after that first day here.

The cool summer nights were quickly being replaced by cold, damp ones. I missed the sun. The light, the warmth, and clarity of daylight. My tan was already fading into a paler yellow-brown.

I finished the sandwich while gazing up at the September half-moon. The woods behind the dorms seemed to be the only places with no lamplight on campus. It felt more natural to have the trees lit up by moonlight, than the artificial brightness of electricity.

Wand at the ready, I closed my eyes, searching deep within myself for a spark of magic. It had to be there. Come on out, magic.

Several twigs snapped behind me. Opening my eyes, I spun around, only to set eyes on Aimes, MacTavish, and Bennett.

My mouth went dry. Had they followed me out here? Why?

"Sorrentino," Aimes said, "what are you doing out here all alone?" His pale green eyes shone with malice.

Bennett snorted. "Looks like she's practicing magic."

MacTavish grinned, sweeping his blond hair out of his eyes, but didn't say anything.

I firmed up my grip on the wand. It was long and pointy, if I had to, I could use it as a weapon. At that thought, my pulse quickened. Seconds ticked by as the three of them stared back at me. Whatever they were here for, it couldn't be good.

"You're weak, Sorrentino." Aimes drew out his clear crystal wand. "You don't need that." With a flick of his wrist, my wand flew from my hand. I moved to retrieve it, but Aimes said, "Stay still."

My feet anchored to the ground. No matter how hard I tried, I couldn't move them. A cold sweat chilled my neck. He was using magic on me and I had no defenses.

"The Council needs someone strong to lead them. That will never be you." Aimes sliced his wand through the air.

My head jerked to the side. Heat and pain exploding in my cheek, like I'd been slapped. I brought my hands up to defend my face. He punched at the empty space in front of him, and I doubled over, winded.

Bennett and MacTavish joined in, using their wands to smack and punch me. Each hit sent both pain and fear coursing through me. My lip split, I tasted blood. I fell to the dirt on my hands and knees.

"Stop," I gasped.

Three distinct strikes laid me out flat. I drew in shallow breaths of air as tears ran down my cheeks. I didn't have to wait for the culling. These three were going to kill me tonight. I moaned, gripping my abdomen, while trying to scoot away from their attack.

Aimes approached. He took a fistful of my hair to yank my head up. "You're done, Sorrentino. Your families legacy is over." He drew his other fist back before crashing it into the side of my face.

The world went black.

When I woke, the pain returned full force. I gasped at the intensity of it and immediately regretted the sharp movement. Moaning, I spit pine needles and dirt from my mouth, but I didn't lift my head or move my body. Everything hurt so much, I couldn't even begin to tell how damaged I was.

I must have lost consciousness again, because I woke with a jolt as sunlight lit the sky in pale greens and blues. Dawn. Sunlight. I could only see it though one eye. The other one seemed sealed shut.

The sound of someone moving through the underbrush had my heart leaping into my throat. A strangled scream escaped me.

"She's over here!" Liam's voice boomed through the woods. The next moment his warm hands brushed the hair from my face. "Caprice, can you hear me?"

A gurgling noise came through my parted, swollen lips.

"Caprice!" Jaxon leaned over me. I peered up at him through my one good eye. His forehead was knotted, and his grey eyes stormed with rage.

Behind him, a giant black wolf appeared. It let out a low, threatening growl, and my breath caught.

"Angel, you're scaring her. Back off," Jaxon said. "We need to get her to the hospital. Give her to me, I'll teleport us."

Liam shook his head. "I think that might be too much for her. I'll fly her."

Jaxon opened his mouth to argue, then snapped it shut. "Go. We'll meet you there." He approached Angel, and they disappeared in a puff of purple smoke.

Carefully, Liam lifted me into his arms. Behind him, I caught a glimpse of reddish-gold wings that matched the color of his hair. Then we were flying through the trees. I wrapped my arms around his neck, biting back a whimper.

When we landed outside the Dean's Hall, Jaxon, and Angel now in human form, were waiting for us.

"Take her to room two." Jaxon matched pace with Liam as he carried me inside. Two nurses and a doctor were in the room already, preparing to treat my injuries.

Liam set me on the bed. "Hang in there."

The medical staff shooed everyone else out. With a wand swish, and a mutter from a nurse, I fell into a deep sleep.

***

The only light in the small room came from the bedside lamp. It wasn't the same hospital room I'd arrived in. This one was furnished to aid in recovery. Several books and a glass of water rested next to the bed. A warm, fuzzy blanket lay across me.

I did a quick mental scan of my body. Both of my eyes opened. My head hurt. I could move my limbs, but a dull ache accompanied the movement.

A nurse came in, he was short and broad-shouldered. "You're awake. Good. How are you feeling?"

"I've been worse. And better." I shifted to sit up, slowly.

"Take is easy. You'll be in here for a couple of days at least." His smile was warm. "There's only so much magic can do, the rest is up to the body. Drink this, it will help."

What I thought was water, turned out to be a pain-relieving potion. It tasted chalky and sweet.

"Do you want something to eat?"

I nodded.

The nurse placed a couple more pillows behind me, then left.

I eased back into the soft down fluff. My mind immediately filled with traumatic memories of Aimes, MacTavish, and Bennett. They were ruthless monsters. My chest tightened. If I told anyone that the three of them did this to me, what would those boys do next? Kill me?

At a couple of new schools, I'd been roughed up a bit before, but nothing like last night. Those witches wanted me out of the way, out of their world. Isabella had warned me about that. And I had no idea what I was going to do about it. Obviously, laying low and ignoring them was not working. They hated my very existence.

The door opened. Instead of the nurse, Jaxon, Liam, and Angel came in. Liam set the tray of food on the nightstand, then sat on the edge of the bed.

Jaxon took a seat on the other side of me, while Angel leaned against the far wall with his hands in his pockets. The three of them gazing at me made my face flush. I remembered how they found me, and my skin heated even more.

"You're looking better, sweetie," Jaxon said, squeezing my hand. The fierceness of his gaze didn't match his words. I knew he was really here to interrogate me about what happened. But I couldn't be mad at him in that moment. If these three hadn't found me... Well, I didn't want to think about it.

Liam took my other hand, startling me. "Can you tell us what happened? Who did this to you?"

Ah, the good cop and bad cop were switching roles today. Though I could never see Liam as a bad cop. He was too sincere.

"I can't," I said. Jaxon's hand clamped down on mine. I knew he wanted to argue, to force me to tell him what happened. For some reason he didn't.

"We really need to know." Liam's thumb stroked my wrist. His voice and his caress sent a soothing sensation through my body.

"I can't tell you." I glanced down at my lap. "They'll kill me if I do."

"They?" Jaxon lifted a brow.

I'd said too much. I pressed my lips together, avoiding their gazes.

"We will protect you." Jaxon shifted closer. "They won't hurt you again."

I narrowed my eyes at him. "You can't protect me. No one can!"

He drew back at my anger.

"What are you going to do? Follow me around all night? Escort me to every class? You can't be with me every minute. And they'll find a way to hurt me."

Liam gave Jaxon a look, like he wasn't being helpful by pressing me on this.

Jaxon sighed, but didn't say any more.

"Caprice." Angel approached the end of the bed. "We will find them. With or without your help. And they will pay for what they've done to you." His eyes had turned that yellow-gold again.

I swallowed hard. A battle of wills with these three was making my head spin. I wanted to give in and tell them. Angel's words held an absolute promise of revenge. I didn't doubt Jaxon's or Liam's dedication to that cause either. But, I couldn't go through another beating like that. I couldn't deal with it emotionally, not to mention physically.

Liam must have sensed my rising panic. "Shh. It will be all right."

He scooted closer, pulling me the last couple of inches into his chest. I let him, feeling his arms wrap about me in the most protective way I'd ever been held.

Tears overflowed down my cheeks. A sob burst through my lips, and I let myself fall apart in his arms.

13

CAPRICE

Aimes, MacTavish, and Bennett acted like nothing had ever happened. They ignored me a little more than usual for the next few weeks, but that was the only change in their behavior. I still refused to tell anyone about them, and Liam, Jaxon, and Angel soon stopped asking.

"I have to get above a ninety-five percent on my mid-terms." Madison sat on her bed, surrounded by textbooks and notepads. "Or mom will give me hell and ride me even harder next term with her idea of daily magical affirmations, and let me tell you that they are not helping! Look at the one she sent today." She waved her wand, making the piece of black paper float across the room to my bed.

I snatched it up. White script words showed starkly against the matte black.

Once you fall into the culling ten percent, there's only a seventeen percent chance that you'll rise out of it.

"If that's not encouraging, I don't know what is." I tossed the note into the trash bin with all the others Madison had already discarded.

Madison sent me an exasperated glance. "She's making me so nervous that I can't focus on my studies. I haven't slept peacefully in like forever, and that's muddling my brain too." She went back to reading the book in her lap.

I was in real trouble with mid-terms. Madison saw how I failed in all the magic-based classes. Over the past couple of weeks she started to talk less about it. Now she hardly ever brought it up. I tried to see it from her perspective. How would I act toward my roommate if I was positive that they were going to be culled at the end of the year?

I wouldn't want to get too close to them, for both our sakes. I might be afraid they'd be a negative influence on me. Mostly, I'd want to protect myself from the eventual emotional grief over losing them.

Scooting off the bed, I smoothed out my grey and black sweater. October had brought cold, wet nights. It was a different kind of cold from Baltimore, more wet and seeping.

I had one more person to turn to before I gave up on my life.

I trekked across the lawn. On a Sunday, I had to hope May would be in her office. A heavy mist hung in the air, and the water particles glimmered in the numerous lamp light. May was nice and much more competent than Ms. Duinn. I should have turned to her sooner.

As soon as I knocked on her office door, she answered it.

"Caprice, come in." May opened the door wide, then closed it behind me. "What brings you in?" Her soft green eyes met mine. A wave of deja vu swept through me and I blinked several times.

"You're related to Liam." I couldn't believe I'd never seen it before now. They were both redheads, but their eye color confirmed the family tie.

May laughed. "Yes, he's my little brother." She sat down behind her oak desk, motioning me to take the seat opposite.

"I'm sorry, I just now realized that. It caught me a little off guard."

"It's fine. Happens all the time."

My brow knitted. "But he's a fae and you're a witch. How..?"

"Ah. Well, our mom's a witch and dad's a fae."

"So you're both only half and half?" I chewed on the inside of my cheek.

"Supernatural bloodlines don't really work like that." She leaned forward, her strawberry hair curtaining her face. "We have both fae and witch blood in us, but one supernatural gene takes dominance over the other. For me, my witch genes are dominant. For Liam, he's a fae."

"So…if you were to have a kid with a…werewolf, then what would the kid be?"

She shrugged. "Either witch, fae, or wolf."

That was kind of crazy. "What about a witch and a human? What would their kid be?"

"Supernatural is always dominant. So the child would be a witch." Her calm green gaze studied me. "Did you come here to talk about genetics?"

"Not really, but it's interesting. I need your help. I'm still trying to figure out how to access my magic, and mid-terms are only a couple of weeks away."

"I assume you already went to your Magic 101 teacher about this?"

I rolled my eyes. "Yep."

May snorted. "Ms. Duinn was my teacher too. I guess she hasn't changed, or become any more useful to her students. So what exactly is the problem, do you think?"

"Honesty, I don't think I'm a witch. But…there is something different—weird." I already liked May. Finding out that she was Liam's sister made me like her even more. And maybe trust her a little. Keeping secrets wasn't working for me. So I dived in.

"A while ago, I tried to practice on my own. Nothing happened with my wand, but my hands felt really warm. Then these black scales covered my hand, and they were glowing like coals…"

She rested her chin in her hands, her eyes growing round. "That's most unusual." May regained her composure. She straightened in her chair. "You're sure your mother was human?"

"I'm not sure of anything. Well, I know that my dad was a witch, but that's all. I don't remember my mom."

"Did Isabella know her?"

I shook my head. "Not personally."

May took in that information with a frown. "Black scales, warm hands, coals. Caprice, I don't want you to use your wand anymore until we have this figured out."

"But what am I going to do about mid-terms?"

"Take them. Although, you'll be excused from the Potions mid-term. I still want you to come to class and do your homework. But, give me some time to look into this. Okay?"

I nodded. Isabella had said that my mom wasn't one of us. Had she meant not a supernatural, or not a witch? I'd have to wait a week to find out...or maybe not.

After excusing myself from May's office, I went to get my phone from the dean. Since that first week, her secretary had taken over handling the checking out and in of student cell phones. Up in the tower, I sent a quick message to Isabella asking for everything she knew about my mother.

A text from Elena popped up on the screen. *OMG! I have a boyfriend. Remember that guy I met at that beach party we went to? The hunky blond dude? Well, he asked me out a few weeks ago and last night we had sex!*

Dread sent a chill over my skin. No, no, no! I knew exactly which guy she was talking about. He was friends with that creep who tried to rape me. The one who'd tried to use compulsion on me. Compulsion wasn't a witch's gift, it was never mentioned in class. My best guess, was it had to be either vampire or fae. Either way, he was a supernatural. Which meant so was the guy Elena was dating.

She was in danger. Who knew what that guy had done to her already. Was she dating him because she wanted to? Or was he compelling her?

I drew a blank on how to explain this to her without telling her about supernaturals. Oh, to hell with it! I texted: *Don't trust him. I can't explain how I know this, but he's either a vampire or a fae. He's not human. You need to get away from him. Remember the creep from the beach who attacked me? They're friends, and he wasn't human either. Please, trust me on this.*

I pressed the send button, then let out a long and colorful string of expletives. The cat was out of the bag now. But I didn't know what else to do. I couldn't ignore the situation and pretend that she'd be fine. Those two guys were supernatural creeps. Predators of the worst kind.

May had excused me from the Potions mid-term exam, so I thought I'd try to get out of the Magic one too. After class on Monday, I stuck around to talk to Ms. Duinn.

"Yes, Ms. Sorrentino? What is it now?" Today her flowy skirt was blue polka dots on a field of yellow.

"My Potions teacher thinks it's dangerous for me to use my wand. She's postponing my mid-term exam in that class. I wanted to know if you would do that too."

"May was always a silly, dramatic girl. There's nothing dangerous with your wand. You simply have no aptitude for magic, so I'd say it's the opposite of dangerous." Ms. Duinn eyed me, it was the most direct look she'd ever given me. "Failure is no excuse for postponement. You will take the Magic mid-term. And don't even think about not showing up, or I'll deduct points from you."

"You'll take points away from my zero?"

"Negative numbers do exist." She turned away.

"But—"

"There are no buts, dear." She called as she left the classroom.

My fists clenched at my sides. She was the worst teacher!

In Potions, May had us pair up. She wanted less advanced witches to watch as a more adept one brewed a complicated protection potion.

"Sorrentino, you'll pair up with Aimes," she said.

The blood drained from my face at the same time my chest clenched in terror. I crossed my arms to hide my shaking hands.

Aimes leered at me.

I stood near enough to his cauldron that it didn't look like I was keeping my distance. Aimes moved past me to get herbs. When he returned, he brushed up against my arm.

In a low voice, he said, "You've been a good girl, Sorrentino. You know we'll kill you—or worse—if you tell on us. Part of me wishes you'd tell, because I really want to do worse." He squeezed my ass.

My yelp was drowned out by the conversations in the room. I wasn't going to turn him in, but I also wasn't going to stand there and take it. I retrieved my backpack from the wall of cubbies.

"Are you all right, Caprice?" May asked, as I headed for the door.

I faced her. "Yes. No. I'm not feeling well. Sorry."

She let me go. Her gaze flicked to Aimes and a frown pulled at her mouth. I hoped she hadn't picked up on what had happened. I darted into the hall.

The lawn was filled with a PE class. I skirted around them, until a tall, dark figure stood in my way. Angel taught PE. I should have guessed that. He was in shorts and a tank top, even though it was only about forty degrees tonight.

"Shouldn't you be in class?" He threw the football in his hands across the field.

"I should be. But, I-I can't right now."

His deep amber gaze pinned me. "Your attackers are witches."

"No!" I said it too fast, and too forcefully.

Angel growled. The sound low and threatening, yet somehow I knew the growl wasn't directed at me. He wanted revenge, for my sake.

"Please don't." I put my hand on his bicep. His muscles tensed under my palm. "Just drop it, please."

"Can't do that."

"Why do you care so much? I'm not your sister, or even your friend. You barely know me."

"No one should ever be treated like that. No one should have to suffer like you did." He took a step back. "I take care of my own."

"But I'm not—"

He jogged into the lawn, shouting, "Blue team, to me!"

Angel was almost as bad as Jaxon when it came to confusing the shit out of me.

May said she was going to look into my scaly skin episode, but I decided to do my own research too. It couldn't hurt. And I hadn't heard anything from her in days.

The library was on the third floor of Sorrentino Hall, which had no windows. Row after row of ten foot tall bookcases seemed to go on forever. At the end of each case, was a plaque stating the subject for that section. The place smelled of dust and old paper.

I gathered books from several sections, including mythology, history, and sociology, plopping the heavy volumes down on a desk. The student at the next table over glared at the loud noise.

"Sorry," I whispered, taking a seat. Their glare deepened. People really took their studying seriously around there.

Black scales, heat, and the look of burning coals. That's what I had to go on, and assuming that it wasn't a disease...and keeping a completely open mind about it...my best guess was salamanders or dragons. Liam had lectured on dragons once. He'd said that they were on the uncertain list. Were they mythological or actual supernaturals?

A part of me balked at that line of thinking. I wasn't a freaking dragon! That would be mind-blowing and impossible. Right? But so was being a witch—at least that was what I'd thought a couple of months ago. For the sake of my investigation though, I was going to keep an open mind until I could rule out the most obvious explanation, given the clues that I had.

For several hours, I dug into those books. It turned out that there was no such thing as salamander supernaturals. And I'd only thought of them because I'd once read about salamanders being associated with fire. So I moved on to dragons. My research reiterated what Liam had said in class. More specifically, no one had seen a dragon-shifter, apparently that was what they were called, in the past several hundred years. Yet, several authors refused to rule out the possibility of their existence because of some old folktales, which were mentioned, but not covered, in the books.

One passage I found particularly interesting...

Dragon-shifters, a rare type of supernatural, choose a home and rarely leave it. As we know from various legends, they adore and collect jewels, gold, and other treasures. They are hoarders. One of their obsessions is protecting their hoard of goods, the other is accumulating more. They are greedy beasts. Female dragon-shifters are rumored to often take several mates.

That passage seemed to rule out dragon-shifter as the answer. I didn't have a home, or mates, or hoard any kind of valuable treasures. I closed the books and put them back on their shelves.

I needed to see May, and at least ask her for an update on her research. She'd know more than me what to look for. My patience of waiting for her to come to me was wearing thin.

In the Academy Hall, I headed toward the hallway that led to the teacher's offices. It was late and the building was quiet. My rubber soles whispered over the stone floor. As I turned the corner at the end of the hall, my feet stuttered to a halt.

May was on her knees in front of an office door, wand in hand. She leaped to her feet as soon as she saw me. Her face turned a truer shade of red than her hair.

"Caprice—I, er, who are you visiting at this hour?"

"You. Unless you're busy." I glanced from her to the plaque on the door. Ms. Duinn. Had May been trying to break into Ms. Duinn's office?

"No, not busy at all. I'm, uh, just over here." She walked the two doors down to her own office.

I followed, entering as she turned on the lights. "What were you doing just now? In front of Ms. Duinn's door?"

May stood behind her desk, her face flaring again. "I was—" she interrupted herself. "Any chance that you could forget that you saw that?" She wrung her hands. Her brow knitted up so tight, it had to be giving her a headache.

I regretted asking about it. I didn't want her to see me as a threat. "Of course. I'm sorry."

Her face relaxed with the relief. "What can I help you with?"

"I just wanted to know if you'd had time to look into my scaly skin thing."

"I'm sorry. I've been so busy with preparing for mid-terms that I haven't yet. I will though, as soon as those tests are done and graded. Okay?"

I nodded, a bit disappointed. Of course she'd have a lot on her plate. Suddenly, I felt selfish for coming to her for an update. "Of course, that's fine. Have a good night." I turned to leave.

"Caprice."

I faced her.

May visibly swallowed, her eyes glistening. "Thank you for..." she trailed off. We both knew what she meant.

I inclined my head before leaving. The desire to know what she'd been up to burned in me. May sneaking around after hours? Trying to break into a fellow teacher's office? That didn't seem like her at all.

14

CAPRICE

Mid-terms at the Academy were unlike anything I'd ever experienced before. My two lecture-based classes had a half night each dedicated to the exam. They were both on the same night, with a long lunch break in between.

I felt good about them, sure that I had aced them both. Spending several hours filling in answers about History and Mythology had been relatively normal and easy. It was tomorrow's exam that I was not looking forward to. I went to bed early, tossing and turning through the whole day.

To make matters worse, I was the last to be called in for the Magic mid-term. Ms. Duinn was not going in alphabetical order this time, probably so that no one could predict when their turn would be up. What was more unnerving was that no one reappeared after they'd been called in to the side room with Ms. Duinn.

Madison spent the two hours leading up to her exam practicing all the spells she'd learned so far that term.

"Where do you think they go?" I asked her. "Is there some other exit in this building?"

"It's a magical test, so I don't think Ms. Duinn wants to risk any of them telling us what the test is. We just need to be prepared for anything and everything." She went back to moving objects around the room, opening and closing the cupboards, and producing first fire then water with her wand. She was so talented.

Ms. Duinn emerged from the smaller side room. "Ms. Swan, you're up next. The rest of you will be served lunch here before we continue."

Madison's lifted her chin as she gracefully walked toward the teacher. I had no doubt that she would do just fine. "Good luck!" I called to her, and Ms. Duinn shot me a brief glare. What? Were students not supposed to wish each other luck? This place was weird. Backward.

Lunch was brought into the classroom on rolling carts. The twenty or so of us left all ate in silence, focused on our inner worlds of anxiety, hope, and determination. I was all anxiety, with no hope at all that I'd get anything other than a zero for this exam, unless it miraculously didn't involve using my wand.

As I nibbled on the club sandwich, my stomach so twisted up that it was difficult to swallow, I focused on my blessings. Aimes and his boys had been among the first to be called in. Which left me with a sense of peace, especially when they didn't reappear. Maybe they'd never return. That was wishful thinking.

I glanced around at the other witches. The first day they'd all been cheering when everyone claimed their wands. Now they kept to themselves, wary of the other students, not really interacting with anyone else. There were a few small cliques that seemed to be confident that they'd all make it out of here alive. They didn't talk to anyone outside of their group.

When passing them on the lawn, I noticed the second years also kept to themselves, but in march larger groups. Avoiding freshmen like they had some contractible disease. I could only imagine how traumatized they all had to be, having just survived their own Culling Year.

It felt like school was becoming an each person for themself kind of battle. How did the teachers live with this? How could they go through each term knowing that several of their students would be fed to canni-bals? Was the Truce really worth all this heartache?

After lunch, and after everyone else had been called in, finally Ms. Duinn came for me. Her smile didn't reach her eyes when she called my name. With a deep breath, I followed her into the side room and tried to brace myself for failure.

The room was not even ten feet in any direction. It held a student desk, and a large leather chair for Ms. Duinn.

She motioned toward the desk. "Sit. You'll have fifteen minutes to complete the written exam."

My heart lifted with hope. I could do a written exam. I might actu-ally do okay on that part, and for once earn some points in this class.

I sat as the teacher settled into the brown chair directly in front of me. Her close presence was distracting from the thick stack of papers on my desk. With effort, I did my best to ignore her and focus on the questions, which were mostly magical theory. I totally had this.

A chime sounded, ending the fifteen minute exam. Ms. Duinn retrieved my papers and they magically disappeared into a pocket on her skirt.

"Now for the practical exam," she said.

My heart sank. "What am I supposed to do?"

"Oh, simple really. I will teleport you to a place where all you have to do is unlock the door to get out. Bye, bye." She flicked her wand, filling the space with purple smoke.

It smelled too sweet, like rotting apples. I gagged and coughed. When I was done sputtering, my eyes opened to dark surroundings. I reached out, only to find a solid wood panel five inches in front of my face.

My palms followed the panel to the corners, then down the sides that were so close I couldn't extend my elbows all the way. I realized I was laying down, trapped inside a box—more like a coffin. I shuddered.

Was I buried alive? What happened if I couldn't unlock this box?

Panic whirled in my gut. I gasped for air. Even though I knew it wouldn't help, I drew out my wand and willed the lock that must be on the other side of the wood to open. When nothing clicked, I started kicking and banging. The thumping of my pulse filled my ears.

Then I screamed.

My voice grew hoarse, my throat raw, as the minutes went by. How many minutes? Or was it hours? The metallic scent of blood filled the tiny space as pain shot through my fingertips. Gasping for the diminishing supply of air, I continued to use my nails to scrape at the wood. I tasted salt as tears ran down my face.

I had to get out. I had to get out. It was all I could think, over and over.

Like a person deranged, I kicked and clawed at the unyielding wooden cage.

"Caprice!" The sound was faint. At first, I wasn't sure if someone was calling my name, or if I was hallucinating it. Then it came again, closer. "Caprice!"

I screamed, the sound coming out dry and cracked. "Here. I'm in here!"

What sounded like a heavy door squeaked on its hinges as it opened. Footsteps clip-clopped on a stone floor to where I was trapped. At least I knew that I wasn't buried underground. The lock clicked, and I shoved against the top, which fell away to the side, letting in blinding daylight.

I stared in horror. I *was* in a coffin.

Strong arms reached in and scooped me up. I recognized Liam's citrusy scent before I focused on his face. His lips her set into a hard line, his brow furrowed.

"Shh. I got you," he said in his most soothing tone as he set me on my feet.

"That bitch!" May stood near the coffin, wand in hand.

"How did you find me?" I croaked.

May's green eyes were livid. "When you didn't appear for dinner... She did the same thing to me my first year." She put away her wand.

My body trembled from the adrenaline. Liam wrapped an arm around my waist to keep me from collapsing. "Aren't there rules against this kind of thing?" I asked.

May came up to me, taking my hands in hers. "There are only two rules here. Don't go beyond the walls. And try not to get culled." That was exactly what Jaxon had said in his office.

"Is that true? I thought it was just a saying." I glanced at my hands and let out a shriek. My nails were broken—torn. My fingers covered in blood.

"Oh, wow. You're in shock." May dropped my hands. "We need to get her to the hospital," she said to her brother.

All I could do was stare at my ruined hands. A wave of dizziness blurred my vision. Liam caught me. He swept me up against his chest, and followed May out the door. He must have been using some kind of fae magic on me, because my body relaxed against him as my nerves settled. The fear and panic subsided to a dull roar at the back of my mind.

The hospital staff had me cleaned, medicated, and bandaged. With a healing potion, they sent me back to my dorm room to recover. It had be around nine o'clock in the morning, and I was not used to being up at that time anymore. Exhausted, I managed to get into my room without waking Madison before collapsing on my bed.

I slept for a good thirty-six hours. Whatever they put in that healing draught had knocked me out. When I woke, I felt good enough to be pissed off at Ms. Duinn for trapping me in a coffin and leaving me there. Knowing full well that I wouldn't be able to get out on my own.

At the same time, I was grateful that it was a Saturday. I chose some fresh clothes, then wandered down the hall for a long, hot bath. I unwrapped the gauze on my fingers, relieved to find that the skin had healed. My nails were still broken but didn't hurt anymore.

The bath did its job to revive me. I was more relaxed than I'd been in weeks as I walked back to my room—until I saw the note tacked to my door. I plucked it off. It was another summons to staff office number nine, which meant having to see Jaxon again.

A whole bunch of feelings hit my chest at the same time. I was still angry with him for trying to bully me the last time I was in his office. A fluttering, that could only be attraction, bubbled up. And guilt, over my unexpressed gratitude for his role in saving me in the woods—twice since I'd arrived in Oregon. Isabella wanted me to trust him, maybe I should. Trusting others was difficult.

The note incinerated in blue sparkles. I gently ran my fingers through my wet hair as I trudged to the staff building and located Jaxon's office. He answered on the first knock, stepping back to let me enter. I could tell from the hard set of his jaw that I was not going to enjoy this meeting.

He strode behind his desk, gesturing for me to take the other chair.

"What? You're not going to harass me at the door this time?" I said before I could stop myself. My anger at him was the dominate emotion at this point. I braced myself for his temper.

His jaw worked, but he didn't have a snarky comeback as I'd expected. Instead he sat down. "I've become aware of your mid-term results in Magic. As your advisor—"

"What? Are you going to stick me back in that coffin? Force magic to come out of my wand?" I gripped the back of the chair that I stood behind. Why did he always make me so mad?

His grey eyes darted to mine. "No. I'm pulling you from Ms. Duinn's class. From now on you'll have private tutoring with me every morning at five. Starting Monday, we'll meet here."

I searched his handsome features. For a moment, I was at a loss for words. He was taking me out of Ms. Duinn's class. That was the nicest thing he could have possibly done for me. I didn't know if he knew that nor not. But it was.

Tutoring with him on the other hand, well... We'd see how that turned out.

"Th-thank you." I managed, when my voice returned.

"It's my job." There was the Jaxon that I knew—all duty. His words dousing the gratitude that had filled me with warmth.

I ignored his tone. "What Ms. Duinn did to me... Are there really no rules here against that sort of thing?"

"No. The teachers are free to do as they wish with their students." He ran his fingers through his blond waves. "The Culling Year is harsh. Teachers don't coddle their students, because it doesn't do any good for anyone. As your advisor, I have the ultimate authority on what is best for your education. That's why I'm taking you out of her class."

"I see."

He held my gaze for a few more heartbeats. "You're free to go. I'll see you Monday." With a flick of his fingers, the door behind me opened. Did he always have to be such a cold jerk?

I stormed out of his office, inhaling deeply to gain control over my temper. I'd worked on that control for years, yet every time I was around Jaxon he pushed me over the edge. I was mad at him for his cold, detached attitude. For his bossy stubbornness. Hell, I was even upset at him for rescuing me. Because he had no right to save my life, and risk his own, when he didn't care about me. Not really anyway.

He made me feel like I was a chore to him. Just part of his job description to look after me, because the queen had ordered him to do so. I was being unfair. That was exactly the situation. I just wanted...more.

Stupidly, I wanted him to like me. I wanted the glimpses of warmth and kindness from him to be genuine. But they weren't.

I stepped into the chilly night air. It was Saturday, which meant I could call Isabella or text Elena.

Shit! Elena. I'd sent her that crazy text last weekend. She must think I'm insane.

I jogged over to the Dean's Hall to check-out my phone. When I turned it on, the low battery warning popped up. As did a text from Isabella and a long message from Elena.

The one from Isabella read: *As far as I know, your mother was human. Hope that helps.*

It didn't help, but I would pass that information along to May.

I thumbed over to Elena's text.

LOL! You're so funny. A vampire? I don't even know what a fae is... His name's Tyler, and he's super sweet. He's not really friends with that guy who attacked you. I guess they were before, but they had a falling out. Tyler is a great guy, you'd like him. So don't worry about me! I'm happy!

I chewed on my lower lip. My best friend was dating a supernatural and didn't know it. He had to have attended Academy Obscura before UMBC, maybe I could ask around about him. See what kind of guy he really was.

Being a supernatural was a huge secret to keep from his girlfriend. Here I was, keeping the same secret from my best friend. Who was in the wrong?

The next day our mid-term report cards arrived under the door of our room. Madison jumped out of bed to retrieve hers, and I did the same. We sat on the floor, and ripped into the envelopes. She scanned the paper inside, sighing with relief.

I read my results and they were as I'd guessed—mostly. Ninety-eight percent in History, ninety-seven in Mythology, and zero in Magic. Ms. Duinn hadn't even given me any points for the written exam part. I never had to deal with her again, I reminded myself. May had even given me a seventy percent just for showing up to class and trying in Potions.

"Did you do good?" I asked Madison.

She grinned and nodded. "Even my mama might be proud of this report. Ninety-eight percent in all of my classes, and I've been working so hard, and it paid off! Maybe she'll stop sending those horrible notes that are supposed to inspire me, now that I have this score. What about you?" Worry creased her brow.

"I'm not doing as well as you, that's for sure. But don't worry about me." I returned to sit on my bed. "Tomorrow I'm starting private tutoring for Magic, so I won't be in class anymore. But I'll see you in Potions."

She gave me a tight smile. I knew what she had to be thinking. Private tutoring was a bad sign. I was going to get culled.

Unless I got the hell out of here first. I had time though. The culling wasn't until the end of the year.

15

LIAM

"You took her out of Ms. Duinn's class?" May asked. She sat on the edge of Jaxon's desk, her hands folded in her lap.

He inclined his head. "Now I need to figure out how to tutor her. How to break past whatever barriers in her mind are in the way of her magic. Any ideas?" Jaxon glanced across his desk at me.

"I think—"

May cut me off. "Has she told either of you about the black scales on her skin?"

"What?" Jaxon and I said at the same time.

"I'll take that as a no." May passed Caprice's story along to us. "I don't think her mom was human. And I don't think that she's a witch. I mean, I had trouble with my magic when I was young, but I could still do *some* things with it. We all knew I was a witch and not a fae."

She had an interesting point. If Caprice's mom was a different kind of supernatural, and the dominate gene...that would explain a lot. However, Caprice hadn't shown any signs of being a vampire, werewolf, fae, or witch...

"Scales you said?" I asked my sister. "Could she be some kind of shifter?"

"I don't believe it at all," Jaxon said. "She burned down her foster families house with fire, which was produced by magic. She's a witch. She's just suppressing her abilities for some reason. Maybe she's traumatized from the experienced."

"That's what I was going to suggest earlier," I mumbled, with a pointed stare at May for interrupting me, which either didn't register or she decided to ignore.

"I think she's a shifter," May said. "But there are so many different kinds. I'm going to do some research. Catch you guys later." She closed the door softly behind her.

"How did my sister get roped into all this?" I asked.

Jaxon shrugged. "For some reason she likes Caprice."

I made a non-committal noise to stop myself from getting on Jaxon's case. It was so obvious to the rest of us that he was in love with Caprice —or at least that he liked her *a lot.* I was fine hanging back and watching him figure it out for himself. Years of experience had taught me that you can't tell Jaxon anything. He'll immediately deny it. Although eventually he always came around, and rubbing in the I-told-you-so was satisfying. But not this time. This time he was on his own to figure it out.

As much as I tried to keep a professional distance with Caprice, she was getting under my skin. Twice I'd carried her battered, traumatized body to the hospital, and while that was absolutely *not* a turn on, it made me feel a greater sense of worth. I felt special being the one to hold her, and help her, and sooth her. Pathetic.

If she had to choose between me and Jaxon, she'd pick Jaxon in an instant. Since he was already in love with her, I didn't stand a chance. All he had to do was realize his feelings, tell her, and that would be the end of it.

Until then, I'd do what I'd promised. Look after Caprice with Jaxon and Angel. Speaking of which…

"What the hell's up with Angel?" I asked. "I thought he was supposed to be helping us with Caprice."

Jaxon stood, rubbing his face. "I don't know. He's been distant lately. Probably a wolf thing."

"Huh." I stood too, glancing at the wall clock. "I have a call to take. See you tomorrow."

I jogged down the hallway, then up the stairs to the building's one tower. It was the only place to get good cell reception, and I had a phone appointment set up with my father. No one else was up there. An early morning sun brightened the heavy, grey clouds. Another wet day was ahead, and a soggy night.

I found his contact in my phone and tapped it. At the first ring, my chest tightened. What did he want to talk with me about? On the second ring he answered with a clipped, "Yes".

"Hi, Father. How are you?" My grip tightened on the phone.

"I heard you're teaching the Sorrentino heir. Is there some reason that you didn't tell me this yourself?" For a fae his voice was gruff.

"I—"

"Don't give me your excuses. It doesn't matter. All that matters is she'll be the next Council Queen, and this is our chance, Liam. This is *your* chance."

I licked my lips. "What exactly do you want me to do?"

"Make her yours, of course. If those damned Stewarts won't die and give up their fae council seat, we'll do them one better and align ourselves with the queen. Your children will rule the supernaturals."

I choked on air. "Father—"

"Don't give me that, boy. No excuses. Compel her if you have to, but get her in bed, and put a ring on her finger. I don't care how you get her. Just get it done." He hung up.

For several moments, all I could do was stare at my phone. My father was always coming up with schemes to displace our family rival, the Stewarts. But this? This was absurd. I had a sinking feeling that he wasn't going to let this one go. He'd call me next week to check on my progress. And what could I do?

With a sigh, I slipped the phone back into my trousers pocket. I'd ignore him. For now. Give my mother time to talk him out of this idea.

Fuck.

I was already his greatest disappointment. This would just be one more of my failures added to the long list he kept. The top among those, of course, was being best friends with the rebel's son. Although, if I didn't follow through with wooing Caprice, this might top all the others.

There was no way I'd use compulsion on her. That was just sick.

Monday morning at five sharp, Caprice arrived at Jaxon's office. She gave me a startled look when I opened the door, then did a quick scan of the room behind me.

"He's not here," I told her.

"But I thought—"

"No. You're right. You have a tutoring appointment. But he agreed to let me...ah...have you for today." That came out way more awkward than I'd intended. I stepped back to let her enter, registering the momentary uneasiness that she felt. I was such an idiot.

"Why? What are we doing?" she asked, setting her backpack in the armchair.

I watched her movements, taking in the curve of her ass and shapely legs. My father's words drifted into my mind. How sweet it'd be to be with Caprice...but that would never happen. If she liked Jaxon even a little, and I was sure she did, then she was his. Not mine.

I shook my head, this wasn't the time to be checking her out. Or indulging in wishful thinking.

She turned to face me, and my gaze slid to her mouth and those luscious—Abruptly, I rounded Jaxon's desk, ready to get to work. Work. That's why she and I were here.

"May thinks that you're not witch," I said, pulling up a case from under the desk.

"Right. We've talked a bit about that." Caprice nibbled on her bottom lip. Jesus. I needed to stop looking at her mouth.

"We're going to do some experimenting today. See if we can figure you out." I pulled a vial from the case. "Here. Smell this."

She leaned across the desk to take a whiff. Her nose wrinkled in disgust. "What is that? It smells like blood."

"It is blood. Human blood. Do you notice any urge to drink it?"

She recoiled. "Ugh! No!"

I stoppered the vial. "We'll rule out vampire."

"You already know I'm not a vampire. We met in the sunlight at the river. Don't you remember?"

I remembered all right. The image of her in cutoffs and a bikini top was seared into my brain.

"Well?" Caprice rested her hands on her hips.

"Of course I remember. But I want to double-check everything we think we know about you. Bear with me." I produced another vial. "Drink this, please."

She gave me a wary glance. "What is it?"

"It's a potion made with fairy dust. It will encourage any fae ability to reveal itself." When she didn't take it from me, I said, "It's just a little prod. It won't hurt you."

She took the vial and downed the contents, her brows rising. "That actually tastes good."

"Fairy dust." I watched her face. "Do you have an urge to spread your wings? Can you sense what I'm feeling?"

Caprice took her time to consider my questions. Her gaze held mine as she tried to read my feelings. Not looking away took all the courage I had.

Finally she said, "No. I don't feel anything different."

"All right. Let's try this one." I handed her another small glass container.

"And this is..?"

"Werewolf. Well, a potion to see if you are one."

"Where'd you get all these?"

"May brewed them."

Caprice smiled. "That was nice of her." She upended the vial, sputtering. "That one's gross!"

"Hm. That should taste good if you're a wolf. Let's give it a few minutes to see if you shift."

"Into a wolf?" Her deep brown eyes widened.

"Well...yeah." I sank into Jaxon's chair as Caprice began pacing the room. Her anxiety rose with each step. "It won't make you shift unless you are actually a werewolf. Since you didn't like the taste, I don't think you are one." I reached out with my calming influence. Trying to sooth her without being obvious about it.

She marginally relaxed, but kept pacing.

I counted to sixty in my head. "Feel anything?"

She halted. "No. What's next?"

"Witch."

"Are you joking?" Her hands returned to her curvy hips.

"Take out your wand. Drink this. Let's see if anything happens." Once she'd done what I told her to do, I came up behind her, hesitantly taking her right wrist in my hand. Her warm skin heated my palm. I swallowed hard. "Hold your wand up, yes like that. Now I want you to focus your intensions on casting a simple spell. I'm going to push my own energy behind yours and see if we can get it into your wand. Okay?"

She nodded.

I closed my eyes to focus on feeling her power, to determine where it was flowing. Her haired smelled like an exotic flower. Mentally shaking myself, I refocused on my task. Her wrist was growing warmer. A pool of energy was backing up into her arm. It seemed that a blockage was in place, not letting her magic enter the wand.

I adjusted my hold on her wrist. With the movement came an

outpouring of her emotions. Lust rolled off of her. It was a heady, light sensation zipping through my mind, that turned southward and shot straight to my groin.

My eyes popped open. I let her go, taking a step back. "Anything?" I asked, my voice strangled. I cleared my throat. "Any magic?"

"No." Her lips were slightly parted in her flushed face.

"Lastly, we have a generic shifter potion." I retrieved it. "Let's hope something happens with this." I handed her the container, then retreated to sit on the desk.

"What sort of thing should happen?" Her anxiety was rising again.

"Nothing big. It should bring out some natural instinct that will clue us in to what kind of shifter you are." I folded my hands in my lap, trying for a casual posture.

Lust? Had I really felt that coming from her? Directed at me? I must have misread her. Angel was right about me. Girls...they didn't respond well to me—or find me attractive. At least not the ones that I was drawn to.

She sipped at the contents before downing the rest. Caprice's eyes became unfocused. She stepped toward me. "Natural instincts? Should I follow them?" Her voice was low and soft.

"Yes. Give in to them. That will give us an idea of what you—"

She lunged at me, closing the distance between us, wrapping her arms around my neck. Her lips took mine in a fiercely passionate kiss. Her fingers swept up into my hair to pull me closer.

Automatically, I grabbed her waist. She squirmed closer, pressing her soft breasts to my chest as she moaned into my mouth. Her tongue parted my lips, plunging into my mouth, caressing and exploring. She tasted like mint with a hint of pineapple. Her lust caught me up in it, and I kissed her back, giving as good as I got. My hands slid down to grip her curvy ass.

The office door burst open. Jaxon's gaze took us in, his face hardening.

I froze.

Caprice nipped at my bottom lip, then turned her head toward Jaxon. "Come here. I want you too."

Jaxon's startled glance met mine. "What did you give her?"

"Just May's potions. I swear." Realizing my hands still clutched her ass, I dropped them to my sides.

"What the—"

May appeared in the doorway. "I think I know what she is."

16

CAPRICE

"Do you have any proof of this wild theory you're presenting?" Dean Wright sat behind her gigantic glass desk. Her gaze flitted from me, to May, Jaxon, Liam, and back again, even though her question was aimed at May.

My face must have been the brightest crimson anyone had ever seen. I wanted to slink away and hide under my bed. I'd *attacked* Liam. A teacher. Like, literally jumped on him and started making out. Then I'd invited Jaxon to join us. Impossibly, my skin heated some more. What had I been thinking?

That was the thing. I hadn't been thinking. I'd done what Liam had said to do. Give in to instinct. He never told me my instincts would turn me into a slut! How embarrassing.

I glanced over at him, immediately regretting it as his ears brightened to match the color of my face. He must be humiliated. Or terrified. I didn't even want to guess what Jaxon thought of me in that moment. And May...

May seemed the calmest of us all. "I don't have any proof. Not yet. But we did run her through several potions of my own making. Her instincts led her to want both Liam and Jaxon. It could be a sign."

The dean's eyes lit with mirth. "I'm sure she's not the only student who would willing take these two to bed."

At that, even Jaxon blushed. It was the first time I'd seen his skin redden. He looked almost boyish, and it was hot. I had a feeling that potion was still messing with my brain.

"And," Wright continued, "it's not enough to prove that she's a dragon-shifter. We don't even know if they exist."

"I know," May said. "All I want is permission to take her out of witch classes and further explore this possibility."

"If she ditches half of her classes, her points will take a fall. Those will be difficult to regain."

"She's already failing both Magic and Potions." May pointed out. "It won't make that big of a difference—at least not negatively."

Dean Wright inclined her head. "I give you my permission. Do whatever you think is best for her. You're all dismissed."

Jaxon and Liam practically raced each other to the door. May wrapped an arm around my shoulders, steering us after them.

"I'm sorry, Caprice, I didn't know that the potion would lead to… that," she said, once we were in the hallway.

I fought another blush and lost. "It's okay. Don't blame yourself. Obviously it's me, not you."

"You shouldn't feel bad." She grinned. "We have a clue now. And we've ruled out all of the other supernatural types. That's some serious progress."

I stopped walking so I could look her in the face. "So, you're not upset at me for practically forcing your brother to make out with me?"

May chuckled. "He certainly wasn't resisting." Her expression sobered. "No. I'm not upset. And as far as what you said to Jaxon…well, dragon-shifters take more than one mate. That's the rumor anyway. That's what clued me in. Besides the fact that you did have a reaction to the shifter potion. Which proves that you are a shifter. We just need to figure out which kind."

"You're so positive about all this." I frowned, lowering my voice. "They just think I'm a slut. Don't they?"

"We don't slut shame around here. Being a supernatural in today's world is hard enough without piling ridiculous morals on top of it." May squeezed my arm. "Besides, if you are a dragon-shifter, you can't help it. So let that word leave your vocabulary. Got it?"

I nodded, chewing the inside of my cheek. "I'm still humiliated. They're teachers. It's so wrong."

"This isn't the human world. We live by different rules here. No one is going to hold anything that happened against you. Trust me. The guys are actually okay. Otherwise, I wouldn't have spent so many years hanging out with them."

"Have you like...you know. I mean not with Liam, because he's your brother, but the other two?" I couldn't help asking, since we were on the topic of sex.

May wrinkled her nose. "Oh, God, no! Jaxon and Angel are like little brothers to me too."

So they could all be mine. I clamped down on that thought, pushing it from my mind. What was I thinking? I didn't really want all three of them, did I? That potion had awakened some strange part of me, and it wasn't going back to sleep.

I switched topics, remembering the other thing I wanted to ask May about. "Which supernatural uses compulsion? And what is it exactly?"

We continued down the hall. "It's a mental manipulation technique that compels a person to often act against their will. Fae are the only ones with the ability. Why do you ask? You don't think Liam—"

"No! Not at all. I know that my throwing myself at him was all me." Besides, Liam was too sweet to use compulsion on me. Wasn't he? I continued with my questions, "Do you know a guy named Tyler? He was probably a student here in the last two years."

"Yeah, he's a fae. I remember him. How do you know him?"

"He's dating my friend back in Baltimore. She's human. I just want to make sure she's safe with him."

May frowned. "Hm. The Council and Tromara don't like us getting romantic with humans. They believe it's dangerous and he could get into a lot of trouble." Under her breath she said, "But what do any of them know." Anyway, Tyler is a good kid. Liam was his counselor and only had good things to say about him."

"Did he have a friend that was not such a good kid? Another fae?"

May eyed me. "Yes. Edwin Stewart. His father holds a seat on the Supernatural Council. That boy was trouble. Fortunately his bad behavior didn't rub off on Tyler. How do you know about them?"

"Oh, just a coincidence." I waved a dismissive hand in the air. "Elena and I ran into them at a University of Maryland Baltimore party last summer. Now she's dating Tyler."

Edwin Stewart. The creep. My chest tightened. If his dad was on the Council, chances were good that I'd run into him again in the future. I shuddered.

Tuesday night, in History, was the next time I saw Jaxon. I sat in my usual seat at the back of class. When I dared to glance up, Jaxon met my gaze. His grey eyes held curiosity, with a hint of uncertainty. I focused on my notebook. My skin flushed. It was so much better when he just ignored me. Especially after what happened in his office.

"Sorrentino." My head jerked up at Jaxon's voice. He motioned me to come up to his desk. Reluctantly, I did as he bid.

He came round his desk, so that his back was to the other students as they filed into the room. I caught a glare from Destiny as she took her seat in the front row.

Jaxon leaned close to my ear. "Let's keep this all under wraps for now. Here's your new schedule. You'll stay in the witches' dorm until we figure everything else out." His breath was hot against my neck, sending a tendril of longing through my chest.

I took the paper from him, then returned to my seat. Earning me another glare from Destiny and her crew. What was their problem today?

The vampire girl caught Destiny's eyes, staring her down.

I unfolded the schedule. In the place of Magic, was tutoring with May. Then for Potions I was assigned as her TA. The guys didn't want anything to do with me, and I couldn't blame them. It hurt though. Neither of them wanted me.

Jaxon lectured on the European Supernatural Council, but I didn't pay much attention. I was too focused on how he avoided looking at me. He'd delivered my new schedule, and once again his duty was done.

Depressed, I packed up my bag and headed to my tutoring session with May. Destiny and her crew caught up with me on the lawn.

"Greedy, bitch," she said. "Going after both Jaxon and Liam." She smirked. "Jaxon hardly looked at you in class. Maybe he doesn't want to fuck a dud witch."

I knew neither Jaxon, Liam, nor May would ever say anything about what I'd done. That left Dean Wright. She must have been overheard talking about me. Now the gossip would be all over school.

My face heated. Maybe I could kill the rumor before it got out of control. "Mr. McIver didn't look at me in class because nothing happened between us. Not that it's any of your business."

Destiny growled. "Everything is my business." She shoved my shoulder—hard. The wolf-girl was stronger than she looked. "And all the hot guys are mine. Until I decide which one to keep. Angel will someday be on the Council, but so will Jaxon. So back off, bitch."

I gritted my teeth. She didn't care about them as people. All she wanted were their positions of power. An urge to protect the guys filled my chest. I fought against it, knowing I should get away from these girls before I lost my temper. But instinct kept me rooted in place.

"You back off!" I shoved Destiny. Catching her off guard, she stumbled. With a snarl, the twins were on me. Each grabbing one of my arms.

Jade screamed in my ear. "Don't you dare touch our alpha!"

Destiny's face flushed with rage. We'd drawn the attention of other students. Several stopped to stare at our showdown.

"Break it up, girls," called Angel. Jade and Amber immediately let me go. Destiny rounded on Angel, snarling. He pinned her with an unwavering glare. For several long seconds they silently battled for dominance. Destiny finally backed down, lowering her eyes to the ground.

With a haughty shake of her head, she said, "Let's go. This trash isn't worth our attention."

The five of them walked away, swaying their hips in the hopes to catch Angel's eye. They had no shame.

I turned to him. "I'm sorry. I shouldn't have pushed her."

His eyes were glowing with that golden light. It should have scared me, but it didn't. Instead, I felt drawn in by his wolfish side. If I was a dragon-shifter, maybe the beast in me recognized the beast in him.

Without a word, he stalked off. Well, to hell with him too. I was so tired of being treated like I was invisible.

I met with May in her office. She flashed me a bright, cheery smile as she closed the door. At least someone was having a good night.

"Are you ready to get started?" she asked, nearly bouncing back to her chair.

"Sure. What are we doing?" I settled across from her.

"Well, I brewed up some more of that potion yesterday—"

"No! Are you crazy?" I wasn't going to go through that again.

She held up a hand. "Hear me out. I want to bring out other natural instincts in you, so that we can get more clues. This is the most direct way to do that."

"But look what happened last time. I don't know." I folded my arms, sulking.

May smirked. "Do you think you're likely to start making out with me?"

"Uh...no." She was pretty, but not at all my type. Not like her brother. "I prefer the man-folk."

"Perfect. Then this should work great." She opened a desk drawer to retrieve another one of those glass vials. "Bottoms up."

I took it from her, swirling the milky yellowish liquid. It didn't look appealing at all. With a cringe, I downed the contents.

Newly familiar sensations rippled through my body. I stood up, suddenly having the urge to return to my dorm room. There was something there that I had been neglecting. Something precious to me and I couldn't wait to get back to it. I headed for the door.

"Where are we going?" May asked, following.

"To my room. I need to go there."

The lawn was deserted, except for a few second year students hovering around the opposite edge. Once we reached my building, I took the stairs two at a time. May kept up, not saying anything, just watching to see what happened.

In my room I went straight to my dresser. I still wasn't sure what I was looking for, until my hand brushed over the old tin lunchbox that I had shoved in there. I brought it to the bed and opened it. A peaceful feeling settled into my stomach.

The tin was filled with seashells. One for each time I'd ventured near enough to the beach while growing up. They were the only long-term, consistent piece in my life and I cherished them. I picked up a smooth shell to remind myself of the texture.

"It worked." May sat down next to me, reaching toward the tin. "And this should—"

I snarled at her. The sound escaped my throat before I even thought about it. I clasped my hands over my mouth, horrified.

"It's okay." Her green eyes were wide, her skin a bit paler than usual. But a smile lifted the corners of her mouth. "I figured that would happen."

"What do you mean?" I returned the shell to the tin and closed the lid.

"Dragons collect treasures. They are very protective of them. The fact that you have these, and your reaction to me trying to take one, are two more clues for us." She bounced on the mattress with excitement.

"But, I read that dragon-shifters collect actual treasure. Like things that have value. These are just old shells."

"I'd imagine it's different for each person. The folktales talk about gold and jewels because they're exciting to us. No one wants to read about the dragon who treasures rocks, or sticks, or crayons. That's just my theory." May reached for my arm. "How are you feeling?"

"I think the potion is wearing off. And...dragon-shifter, really? That creeps me out more than being a witch. What am I supposed to do with that?" If I was actually a dragon-shifter, so rare that most people though they were myth, who was supposed to teach me how to be one? I'd roared at May, it had been an instinctual reaction. What was I actually capable of? For the first time in my life—no, for the second time—I was afraid of myself.

The first time was when I'd, maybe, burned down my foster family's home. If only I could remember what had happened leading up to that. Vague images, almost feelings of trying to protect someone always crept up, along with screaming at my foster dad. Then the flames and accusations. But that was all. Those three images ran in a loop.

My pulse sped and my breath caught as soon as I entered Liam's classroom. I ate up the sight of him. That silky red hair, his smooth freckled skin over hard muscle, those full lips. Now that I'd tasted those lips, I hungered for another chance to have his mouth on mine.

What was happening to me? I'd never been this horny for someone before. And he was a teacher—off limits, at least in my rational mind.

As I sat in the back row, his soulful eyes darted to mine then away. The tops of his ears reddened—which only made me want him more. And I was sure he could feel all the lust flowing off me.

God, this was embarrassing.

As he started his lecture, his voice seemed to caress my skin. The deep, soft resonance sunk to my core. I squirmed in my seat. Liam blushed at the front of the class, momentarily faltering in his delivery. I was torturing him as much as he was unintentionally tormenting me. He cleared his throat before continuing.

For the next forty minutes we stole glances at each other. The other fae students openly smirked as they read our emotions. Liam sped through his lecture to stay focused. I'd never seen him so nervous before. Watching his reaction to my emotions only fueled my lust, my heart hammering against my ribcage.

By the time class ended, my panties were soaked, my skin flushed. This dragon-shifter crap was a real problem. How was I supposed to get through the rest of term? How was Liam supposed to focus with me in his classroom?

The class emptied out as I packed up my bag. To my surprise, Liam started to approach me. I couldn't let that happen. If he got within five feet of me, I was going to jump his bones whether he wanted it or not. My dragon side would devour him.

He parted those mesmerizing lips. "Caprice—"

I grabbed my backpack and sprinted out the door. The next few weeks of being around him were going to be blissful hell. Or was it hellish bliss?

First thing Saturday, I was on the phone to Isabella. It was early enough in the evening that I had the turret to myself for once. After catching her up on the whirl-wind of a week I'd had, there was a long silence.

"Dragon-shifter?" Isabella asked. "May is convinced of this?"

"She is. But the dean isn't. Not yet anyway." I fidgeted with a loose thread on my sweater. "Well, what do you think? I mean, is it really possible?"

"Caprice, I'll love you no matter what kind of supernatural you are. I want you to know that."

I sighed in relief.

She continued, "It is possible. It would mean that your mother was a dragon-shifter. I never knew...I wonder if your father knew..." Her voice trailed off as she thought about it. "No, he would have told me if he'd known."

"Do you think that I have more family in Cyprus? Other dragon-shifters?" The idea terrified and thrilled me.

"That would be more than likely. I'll contact the European Council and have them start searching for that side of your family. It's the least I can do for you."

She was feeling guilty again for pulling my mom and dad apart. I didn't want to make it worse for her or rub it in. But if she'd known my mother was a supernatural, would my parent's have had her blessing? It didn't matter now. There was no changing the past.

"Thank you, grandma."

"Of course. Now I have Lyra Gataki as your mother's name. Do you know anything else about her?"

"No. Just her name on my birth certificate. She didn't even have a drivers license," I said.

"Well, that's a start. I'll see what I can find out."

"Really, thank you. That means a lot to me. All of your support does."

"You'll always have it. Oh, Caprice, let's keep this dragon-shifter news quiet. It's going to cause quite a stir in the community once we announce it. I want to plan the announcement for it, rather than have the gossips latch onto the news. Fair enough?"

"Of course. May and the guys are keeping it on the down-low on campus too." I glanced out the long slit window. Rain pounded the Academy grounds. "How do you think the other supernaturals will react to this?"

"I don't know exactly. Rediscovering another type of shifter after several hundred years will be note worthy. Dragon-shifters will have to be recognized and given the chance to run for the elected council position. Not to mention integrated into our society, if there are any others here in America."

That was a disturbing thought. I could be the only dragon-shifter in the United States.

After saying our goodbyes, I checked for texts from Elena. She'd sent one: *Miss you!*

17

CAPRICE

"Dean Wright won't let you switch supernatural tracks until we can either get those scales to appear again, or you shift into your dragon form." May stood over a small black cauldron, stirring as it bubbled. A slight frown pulled at her lips. "This one has got to work."

I leaned against her workbench in the Potions classroom with a sigh. It was just the two of us, and the large stone room felt drafty and cold now that winter had fully set in. December in Oregon was very different than Maryland. More damp and dreary, with less snow.

I eyed the cinnamon-scented brew. It had been weeks since the potion had revealed any more of my dragon-shifter instincts. I felt stuck in this limbo. Any type of supernatural training was on hold until we had this figured out and could convince the dean.

"You think this concoction will work?" I asked May.

Her hair had frizzed with the humidity. "I've made it as strong as I dare." At my expression, she continued, "Don't worry. It can't hurt you. The worst would be an upset stomach." She dipped her wand into the brew, holding a vial in her other hand. As she magiced the potion into the container, the vial slipped from her fingers. It make a plop sound as it disappeared into the cauldron. "Damn!" May muttered. She reached for another of the glass containers, which fell over and skittered across the table.

I caught it before it crashed to the floor. "Are you okay? You seem distracted."

"I'm fine." Her frown deepened. "It's nothing for you to worry about. Here." She filled the vial, then held it out to me expectantly.

I took it, draining the contents that tasted like fire whisky. It burned down my throat to settle in my stomach. Some of the chill in my bones retreated.

We waited. And waited, and waited.

"Anything?" May asked, leaning closer.

"I feel warmer," I offered, as unhelpful as that was. The many potions had awakened enough dragon instincts in me that they'd integrated with my personality. Which was part of the reason I'd been avoiding Jaxon and Liam. Coming to class as late as possible and slipping out as soon as the bell rang. Angel, thankfully, kept a distance all by himself. Each time I drank more of May's brew, the effects seemed diminished.

She let out a frustrated grunt. "I don't know what else to do."

"Should I maybe talk to one of the shifter teachers? Maybe they know something about shifters that you don't." I didn't mean to sound ungrateful, but I'd been wondering for some time if being tutored by a witch was the problem.

May waved a dismissive hand. "Most shifters begin morphing naturally when they're fifteen or so. Since you haven't, I don't know what more they could do for you." She pursed her lips. "I feel like the problem is within you. That some part of your subconscious is resisting the shift. Did anything traumatic happen when you were about fifteen?"

I chewed on my lip. Jaxon and Isabella were the only two who knew about the house fire. Could May be right? Was I blocking myself?

"Something did, yes."

"I think that's the key then. Why don't we let Liam use his fae abilities to unlock your mind?" She glanced at the wall clock. "It's almost lunch time. We could track him down."

"I'd rather...try on my own first." The last thing I wanted was Liam wandering around in my head. Or spending time alone with him. My skin flushed just thinking about that.

May frowned again, but nodded. "Okay, but we need to get this resolved before next term starts. I want you enrolled in shifter classes."

I had a week before finals week, followed by two weeks of winter break. Plenty of time to convince myself that breathing fire and shifting into a dragon was okay. Right?

The Saturday after finals week, all the first year students were gathered in the Dean Hall's giant lobby. The magical scoreboard had been erected, but it was still blank. Any time now our names would appear with our first term points next to them. This was the moment some of us had been anticipating and others dreading. I just wanted to see how far down the board I was, to determine how far I had to climb up next term.

I still hadn't had any luck with shifting my form. Every time I thought about giving up and going to Liam, my stomach twisted in knots of embarrassment—or were they knots of anticipation? No, I had to figure this out on my own.

Madison fidgeted beside me. "What do you think is taking so long?"

"If it means getting the results right, they can take all night for all I care." I glanced around at my follow classmates, wondering which ones were failing. Some of these people would be gone—dead or worse—in another six months. I might be among those. I suppressed a shudder.

The scoreboard lit up. Starting at the top, row after row of names filled in. Madison let out a whoop when her name was listed.

Almost at the bottom a red line appeared to occupy one row. Below that line, more names were added.

Second from the bottom was mine.

I was way low in the ten percent. My head spun. For the first time, my situation was sinking in. This was real. This was life or death. And this system was arranged so that death was inevitable. There had to be a culling.

"Guess that puts you in the Culling Club, Sorrentino." I jumped at Aimes' voice right behind me. My pulse pounding in my ears. "Another Italian witch bites the dust."

"I'm not—" I cut myself off. It wasn't common knowledge that I wasn't a witch. Not yet. And Aimes was the last person I wanted to know about that.

I turned to Madison. "What's the Culling Club?"

She stared at me with those big doe eyes. "I'm sorry, Caprice, but I just can't—" Unshed tears glistened. She turned away, her long legs taking her into the crowd.

Aimes still watched me, with his arms folded over his broad chest. MacTavish and Bennett were chatting up some other witches about ten feet away.

"The Culling Club," he said, "is formed every year for those under that big, red line on the board. It's to honor those who sacrifice themselves for the Truce." He licked his lips. "The Club is a place to party, drink, fuck. What are you going to do with the last six months of your life, Sorrentino?"

I cringed away from him. I was going to get above that line. Somehow.

Aimes chuckled, turning he joined up with the rest of his group. Now that the board was up and everyone knew where they stood, the hall was emptying out. I didn't want to be left alone with the witches, but I didn't feel like going back to my room and a distant Madison. Instead, I headed to May's office. She might be in.

I knocked several times on her door. When I was about to give up, she tore it open. Her face red with anger, and tears streaming down her cheeks.

"What's wrong?" I asked, stepping toward her.

She turned away. "Nothing. Everything." She sniffed. "How did you score?"

I stood staring at her back. I wanted to cry too, for my own reasons. Showing up below that red line made me feel like I'd failed May. She'd worked so hard to help me.

"Not good," I finally said.

"We'll figure something out. Try not to worry about it too much." She snatched up a tissue from her desk and blew her nose.

"Do you want to talk about it? About whatever is upsetting you?" I chewed my cheek, torn between staying to offer my support, and feeling like an intruder on her personal life.

May met my gaze. Her green eyes sad and worried. "I'm not going to burden you with my own issues. What did you come to see me about? Your score?"

"I was actually hoping to be distracted from my score. But I'll do that someplace else."

"You have two terms left. A lot can happen in that time. Okay?" With shaky hands she wiped at her damp cheeks.

I wished she'd let me in. Tell me what had her so angry and sad. I quietly closed the door as I left, feeling so very alone.

———

Winter break was always one of the worst times of year. It meant spending too much time with my foster families, odd gift exchanges, and forced merriment. I had a feeling that this one was going to top the list as the worst of all time.

We were stuck on campus. Just the first year students with minimal staff left to make sure we didn't destroy the place. The Academy felt like a ghost town, especially in the dead of night as snow drifted onto the lawn.

Without classes or homework, I had way too much time to think. I leaned against a lamp post watching the snow fall. My life had just begun a few months ago. I was eighteen and out of the foster system. Finally I could be in charge of my own life. Or not. Instead, I'd ended up in a freak show college, lined up for the slaughter.

I was going to die. To be fed to the Tromara.

Every day I thought about that. Every day hopelessness nestled deeper into my chest.

If I left here, and the Tromara found out about it, they'd kill Isabella. If I stayed, I was doomed. Madison's mom's note also kept popping into my brain. *Once you fall into the culling ten percent, there's only a seventeen percent chance that you'll rise out of it.*

I was fucked.

A shiver ran through me that had nothing to do with the dropping temperature. I headed back to my dorm, not at all looking forward to Madison's cold shoulder.

When I entered our room, she held out an envelope but didn't meet my gaze. "This came for you."

"Thanks." I opened it. Inside was an invitation to a Culling Club party tomorrow night. The idea of a party made me miss Elena. We'd had plans to party our way through college together. Another unfulfilled goal.

Now that she had a boyfriend and had settled into life at UMBC, she wasn't as responsive to my text messages. My old life was really fading away.

I glanced at Madison. "This is an invitation for a party tomorrow. Want to come?"

"No thanks." She remained focused on the book in her lap.

We spent the rest of the night ignoring each other. The one good thing about all this downtime was it allowed me to read another classic novel, this time *The Strange Case of Dr Jekyll and Mr Hyde,* and check it off my list. Though, the storyline was particularly disturbing given my current struggle with my identity.

I woke to Solstice evening. Making my way down the hall to the bathroom, I noticed someone had magiced strands of lights all along the ceiling. They floated about six inches from the top with no visible strings. It did little to improve my mood.

Back in my room, Madison was awake too. For the first time since the scoreboard had gone up, she grinned when I came in, chucking a package at me.

"My mama sent you cookies," she said. "And I know you'll love them because she's the best baker I've ever met. You have to open it and try one. Oh, and those are for you too. They appeared just a moment ago on your bed."

I glanced at my bed, where, sure enough several wrapped packages sat atop the crumpled blankets. The tags showed that they were from Isabella. I brushed my fingers over the silver and green patterned paper. Receiving gifts always made me feel awkward.

"Tell your mom thanks for me, will you?" I asked Madison. She nodded, tearing into her own gifts.

I picked through my small pile. The three packages were from my grandma. There were also several envelopes that were unmarked. I opened one at random, which turned out to be from May, wishing me a happy Yuletide.

The second one I plucked up was from Jaxon. My heart skipped a beat.

Don't give up, Caprice. We'll get you out of the culling next term. You have my word. And happy Yule. -Jaxon

This school didn't have any rules against showing favoritism, it seemed. For a second, anger flared in me. It was fine for all the other kids to die, but I was getting special treatment for being Isabella's granddaughter. It was unfair. At the same time, I was grateful. And that made me feel horrible about myself.

The last card was signed by Liam. Heat flooded my cheeks. I'd kissed him. It had been amazing. A hunger stirred in me at the thought of him, and I had to resist the urge to seek him out. At least I could control these crazy dragon-shifter instincts—for the most part.

His card was disappointing. *Happy Yule. I hope you have a good holiday. -Liam*

I didn't want to think too much about him at the moment. A break from him was good, just what I needed to clear my head. Right?

The first package I opened was a hand-knitted sweater in deep red and black. I rubbed the material against my cheek, surprised at its softness. Next I unwrapped a variety of books that were on my to-read list. She'd sent *Lolita, Brave New World,* and *Atonement.* Isabella knew me better than I'd realized.

The last, and smallest gift, had a hand-scrawled note attached to it. *Of all the family heirlooms, I thought this was best to pass on to you now. May it bring you good luck and courage.*

Curiously, I tore open the small package to find a velvet covered box. It opened on tiny hinges, inside was a dazzling ruby suspended on a gold chain. My breath caught. It was the most beautiful thing I'd ever seen.

Madison craned her neck, catching my eye. "What do you have there?" she asked.

I held the box toward her so she could see it.

"Oh my God!"

"Yeah, that was my reaction too." I brushed my fingers over the sparkling jewel, as I stared at it in awe. This necklace had to be worth a fortune. It was too much. I snapped the box closed.

"Aren't you going to put it on?" Madison asked. "A piece like that shouldn't live in a box."

"It's safer in there." Wearing it would make me feel like I was pretending to be someone else. Some rich person who could put on a jewel like that and act like it was normal. That wasn't me.

The Culling Club party was held in the basement of Sorrentino Hall, which was also the club's headquarters. I'd decided to dress up a bit with a blouse and mini-skirt, because why not? Who cared that it was freaking freezing outside.

As I surveyed the party-goers, I wondered which of them were among the twenty who would be culled. And, if I managed to dig my way out of the club, which student would then take my place.

I downed the beer in my hand, apparently underage drinking was also not a big deal at this school. Why would it be? Everyone here was either going to die or have to watch others die at the end of the year. This whole situation sucked. Did I sacrifice myself or someone else? Those seemed to be the only two options in this warped supernatural world.

The basement was packed with what looked like most, if not all, of the first year students. When I'd entered, I'd spotted Aimes with his group on one side of the room and so far managed to steer clear of them.

I refilled my beer cup, drinking in the hoppy tanginess. I wasn't sure if it was thoughts of mortality, or the holiday season, or that necklace that Isabella had given me, but I was in a dark mood tonight. I chugged the rest of the beer and went for another refill at the keg.

Pop music competed with the roar of voices as people shouted into each other ears. I took up a post against one wall, tapping my foot to the beat. The beer was finally starting to drown out my feelings and thoughts. I welcomed it.

Madison entered with a group of witches. So she had been planning to attend, just not with me. I tried to brush off the hurt that swelled in me by taking another swallow, only to realize that my cup was empty again. I pushed through the crowd to get back to the keg.

Two more beers and I was out on the dance floor, just trying to blend in with the other writhing bodies. Letting the music take over, I danced like I didn't have a care in the world. No culling, no bullies, no dragon-shifter shit. I was free.

Strong hands grabbed onto my hips from behind, moving in rhythm with me. They pulled me in to grind up against a solid, hot body. An even hotter erection pressed against my ass. I smirked, wondering which guy I was dancing with.

"You're so hot, Sorrentino."

A chill prickled my scalp, momentarily sobering me. I turned my head to find Aimes' cruel emerald eyes heated with desire. I stopped moving, trying to break free of him.

His grip tightened on my hips. "Oh no, you're not going anywhere. Tonight you're mine." His beer-scented breath prickled the fine hairs on my neck. My chest clenched as a cold sweat chilled my skin. "Be a good girl and come quiet, and I won't hurt you."

I nodded and he let me go, taking my hand in his.

I rounded on him, shoving my knee into his groin as hard as I could. He went down fast, his face contorted in agony. I pushed through the crowd toward the exit. Climbing the stairs, my pulse pounding in my ears, I made it out the door that opened into a quiet, freezing night.

My head spun. I used the side of the building for support, resting my forehead against the cool stone. My limbs felt wobbly, partly due to adrenaline, but mostly from alcohol.

I had to get out of there and back to my dorm. I shuffled along the side of the building, both hands planted on the rough surface to keep my balance. It took forever to reach the corner. When I did, I slipped around the side and slid down to sit on the damp grass.

This was not good. Fear and nausea fought for dominance in my stomach. I had to…find help. But everyone was back there at that party. Now I was alone.

Footsteps crunched on the gravel path in front of the East Hall. They were coming closer to where I sat. I tried to stand, but the world tilted. I fell back down and landed hard on my ass.

"There you are." Aimes rounded the corner. His eyes hard, his jaw clenched, as he leaned down to yank me up by the arm. One of his hands twisted into my hair. He used it to pull my head back, his mouth coming down on mine hard.

I screamed. Someone had to hear me. It was my only hope.

Aimes tsked. His wand appeared in his other hand. He pointed at my throat and murmured a spell.

I screamed again, but this time no sound came out.

I grasped my throat in horror. He'd silenced me! No matter how hard I tried, no sound would come out of my mouth.

"That's better." Aimes put away his wand, his free hand coming up under my shirt to fondle my breasts. His mouth moved to my chin and neck.

I beat against his chest. Tried to knee him again, but he pinned me to the side of the building with his body. I was trapped, dizzy from too much beer, and completely unable to fight him off or call for help.

A gasp escaped me when he shoved my skirt up to my waist. He parted my legs with a forceful thigh. I silently whimpered against his shoulder.

He drew back a couple of inches to unfasten his pants, letting them drop to his ankles. He used the hand he had wrapped in hair to pull my face to his. "I have to show you your place, Sorrentino." He stared into my wide-eyed gaze. "You're in the Culling Club because you're weak. You're nothing. I'm going to make you my play-thing until the end. Now I want you on your knees." He shoved me down to the ground.

A long, low growl broke through the quiet night air.

I silently yelped as Aimes was yanked away from me, his hand still twisted in my hair. I slumped against the cold stone wall. Through my hazy vision, I registered that Jaxon and Liam each took one of Aimes' arms.

Aimes struggled against them. "Get off me! Let me go."

Angel, in human form wearing only jeans, came around in front of Aimes. He punched him in the stomach. Aimes doubled over. Then Angel grabbed his hair, punching him again, this time in the face. Aimes slid to the gravel unconscious.

18

CAPRICE

"I'll deal with him," Angel said. "Take care of her."

Jaxon and Liam both rushed to my sides. Liam took one of my shaking hands in his, as the other wiped tears from my face. Jaxon pulled my skirt down to cover my underwear. His grey eyes bright with anger.

"Did he hurt you?" Liam whispered, brushing a strand of hair behind my ear.

I opened my mouth to answer, but not sound came out. I clawed at my throat.

"That bastard." Jaxon took out his wand. I'd never seen it before because he always used his hands to direct his magic. The tapered stone was orange and red carnelian. He pointed it at my neck to removed Aimes' silencing spell.

I gasped. "I think I'm okay." The words came out slurred. Then I leaned to the side and vomited. Liam held my hair back.

"Okay," Jaxon said. "Let's get her home." Once I'd finished puking, he scooped me into his arms. Liam walked ahead of us on the lawn, opening doors as we came to the Academy Hall and went up the stairs. Apparently *home* meant Jaxon's apartment.

The space was plush yet masculine. He had more furniture than I would have expected in a bachelor's apartment. Even matching sofas and a coffee table in the living room.

My eyes started to water. "I think I'm gonna be sick." I told Jaxon, who carried me straight to the bathroom and set me in front of the toilet. I heaved into it, feeling ashamed and disgusting. After tonight, none of these three were going to want anything to do with me. I tried to tell myself that would be a good thing, and make my life simpler.

I groaned. Jaxon handed me a glass of water. I rinsed my mouth with it then drank the rest. My stomach settled a little. "Thank you," I murmured at him.

He left me alone for a few minutes. I blew my nose in a tissue. Finding a bottle of mouthwash on the counter, I rinsed my mouth again. My hands were still shaking. I glanced into the mirror and cringed. Then went to work wiping the runny mascara from under my eyes.

Aimes had tried to rape me. The reality of it settled over me and I vomited into the sink. Was I puking because of the booze or because of what I'd just been through? Probably both. I shuddered.

I rinsed out the sink, and my mouth—yet again. I was safe now, with Jaxon and Liam. At least I hoped I was. Irrational fear fluttered into my chest. Or was it irrational? I shook my head. I had no reason not to trust these two. They'd saved me from Aimes.

"Okay, cupcake, do you think you're done retching?" Jaxon stood in the doorway behind me.

I met his eyes in the mirror. "I think so."

"Come on then, let's get you to bed." He wrapped an arm around my waist as I stumbled out of the bathroom. Steering us toward an open door, he flicked on the light. We stood in his bedroom. A massive king size bed dominated the space. The sheets were turned down.

"In you go." He lifted me and set me under the covers. "If you need to puke again, there's a bucket right down here." He left, closing the door behind him.

I snuggled into a pillow that smelled like spice and oatmeal soap.
More than that, it smelled safe and familiar.

The nightmare was back. I sat in a dark room with filthy brown carpet.
A mattress in the corner for a bed. A man shouted downstairs. "Clumsy
bitch! Deserves the belt!" Panicked, I ran down the hall to the stairs. In
the living room, a little girl was crying. A woman cringed against the
far wall. The jingle of a metal buckle sounded at the man took off his
belt.

When I woke with a start, the clock on the nightstand told me I'd
slept through the day. I lifted my head, but when the room spun, I set it
back on the pillow. The events of last night came rushing back to me. I
groaned, turning to lay on my side.

What was Angel going to do with Aimes? Surely, they had some
rule against rape in this damned place. I didn't want to think about
Aimes. All it did was fill my stomach with revulsion.

I was in Jaxon's room, in his bed. A pleasant tingle ran through me
as I breathed in his scent. Then I remembered more of last night. Of
puking my guts out, looking like shit, and Jaxon putting me to bed. My
face heated. How freaking embarrassing. This was way worse than
making out with Liam and inviting Jaxon to join it—which was the last
time the three of us had been in the same room together. Well, there
was having to explain everything to the dean.

Humiliated. That's how I felt. I wished I could sneak out of this
room and hide in my dorm. But at some point I'd have to face Jaxon,
and maybe Liam and Angel too. They'd pulled Aimes off of me. Would
they know that it was him and his friends who'd beat me up? Either
way, whatever they did to Aimes, he would blame me for it. And take it
out on me later.

The bedroom door opened. Jaxon walked in, wearing only his
jeans. Dear God, he was gorgeous. He thrust a glass of water and

several aspirin into my hands. I swallowed the pills. He was a good man. Too good for me.

"How are you feeling?" He sat at the edge of the bed.

"Um." My face flared.

Jaxon reached out and caressed my cheek. The gesture lessened the harshness of his voice as he said, "Don't you dare blame yourself for what happened last night. That wasn't your fault in any way. Do you understand me?"

I couldn't help it, I let out a sob. Those were the exact words I needed to hear. Even though did blame myself for being so careless.

Jaxon scooted closer to pull me against his chest. "I've got you. You're safe now," he murmured against the top of my head.

I let myself cry into his bare chest. The warmth of his skin sunk into my very core as the headache eased. Once I cried myself out, Jaxon wiped away the tears from my cheek with his thumb.

He bent his head close to mine. His lips brushed against the corner of my mouth in the most gentle kiss. Then he drew back with a sigh. His grey eyes held my gaze for a long moment. I read in them everything that he wouldn't say. Fear and longing. What did Jaxon fear? What did he long for?

"Knock, knock." Liam stood in the doorway, holding a bundle of fabric. His gaze took us in. Not a flicker of jealousy registered, though I'd been tense and ready for it. "I brought you a change of clothes." He strode in and set the bundle at the foot of the bed. "You can shower and change in there."

I glanced at a half-open door across the room that must lead to a second bathroom.

Jaxon stood, leaving the room with Liam. They closed the door behind them.

In the bathroom, the scent of oatmeal soap was what I noticed first. The space was smaller than the other one, with a shower stall, sink and toilet. It had the same gleaming white tile.

I peeled off last night's outfit. The skirt and shirt felt dirty, violated. I never wanted to see them again.

The corner unit shower held shampoo, shaving cream and razor, and that signature soap bar. I lathered up in it, fine with being covered in Jaxon's scent. I let the hot water beat down on my skin. It was a start to washing away the horror of last night.

Dried and refreshed, I pulled on a familiar pair of jeans and sweater. Liam must have gone into my room to get my clothes. I cringed. Madison was sure to have something to say about that.

I slipped back through the bedroom, then out to the main room in fuzzy-socked feet. Three gorgeous guys glanced up at the same time. I didn't know what to say to them. They'd saved me from an awful situation last night. They'd taken care of me when I'd been beat up and left in the woods. A tender spot in my heart for each of them fluttered through my chest.

"Thank you." My voice came out stronger and steadier than I'd anticipated.

They inclined their heads.

"How about some food?" Liam asked.

Angel headed for the kitchen.

"That would be great. Thanks," I said, as Jaxon took my elbow, steering me to the table.

Liam set out plates, while Angel retrieved the food that had been keeping warm in the oven. Pancakes, scrambled eggs, and sausage links were placed on the table. The aroma made my mouth water.

Everyone sat down and silently dug into the food. Jaxon poured coffee for me first, then filled everyone else's cups.

I watched them all eat. Jaxon shoveled breakfast into this mouth like a teenaged boy. Liam ate in small bites, giving me a subtle smile when he caught my eye. I was rewarded with a wink from Angel. Which was the most direct interaction I'd had with him in weeks.

These three were so comfortable together. Just being in their presence made me feel more relaxed. May had said they'd grown up together. Had they always been close like this? From what I'd seen on campus, the supernaturals seemed to hang out with their own type. What drew together a witch, a fae, and a werewolf?

Liam grinned. "You're curious about something. What is it?"

I blushed at his attention. "How did you three become friends?"

They exchanged a glance. Jaxon spoke up, "My father led the last rebellion against the Tromara. Many people died because of him." He cleared his throat. "And some of them took out their anger on me. When I was nine, a few older kids were beating me up. Angel came and fought them off. Liam stepped in too, but I think he just felt sorry for the poor lonely son of a hated man." Jaxon frowned, as if he didn't like telling that story.

"I can't imagine anyone beating you up," I said.

Angel snorted. "He was a beanpole. Such a scrawny little kid."

"I can't picture that at all." I sipped on my coffee.

"We have pictures." Angel started to stand up.

"Don't you dare!" Jaxon glared at him.

Liam chuckled. "You'll have to take our word for it. Anyway, after that we fell into an unexpected friendship. And we've been close ever since. Honestly, I think it's because the three of us are all kind of outcasts."

"Oh? How?" I would ask questions for as long as they'd let me.

"Well, I started rebelling against my father. Being friends with Jaxon really put it to the old man."

"That's a great reason for our friendship," Jaxon said sarcastically. "Thanks for that."

"And Angel..." Liam glanced at the werewolf. "Why the hell are you friends with him?"

"Someone needed to protect his scrawny ass, and you weren't going to do it." Angel sat back with his arms crossed.

Redness was creeping up Jaxon's neck. "Shut up. Both of you."

I smiled into my mug.

Jaxon changed the subject. "You're welcome to stay here as long as you'd like, Caprice. When you're ready to go back to your dorm one of us will escort you."

My good mood faded. "I, um—what happened to…"

Angel answered my incoherent question. "Dean Wright stripped him of his points. He's now in the culling."

I gaped at him. "In the culling? With me?"

"That does put you both in the same club. But you won't be seeing him. The dean also took away all of his activity privileges—including Culling Club events."

"So she took away his points and his privileges. For trying to fucking *rape* me? How is that justice?" I set the mug down with a thump.

Liam reached across the table for my hand. I pulled away.

He said, "It's all we can do. The Tromara won't let us punish our own criminals. Criminals have to be presented at the end of year culling. In the meantime, all we can do is limit their ability to interact in society."

"Like put them in a prison cell?" I thought that sounded like a great idea. What the hell was wrong with this place?

"We don't have a jail on campus. And he can't leave the school, as per the terms of the Truce."

"I know a nice coffin we can stick him in," I mumbled, crossing my arms.

"I fucked him up good," Angel said. "He won't be in any condition to hurt anyone for quite a while."

I nodded. At least that was something.

Angel eyed me. "He was the one who beat you up and left you in the forest, wasn't he?"

I lowered my eyes. I'd kept the truth of that from them because I was afraid of what Aimes would do to me if I told anyone. I was so stupid. I'd kept quiet, and that had only shown Aimes that he could do anything he wanted to me and I'd never tell on him.

Jaxon squeezed my arm. I glanced into his angry grey eyes. "Is that true? Was it him?"

"Yes. I'm sorry."

"It's not your fault." Jaxon's voice softened. "You were doing what you thought was right."

"Even so, it is my fault. If I'd told you sooner..."

Angel asked, "Was it only him?"

I swallowed hard. I was about to ruin the lives of two other boys. Boys who'd used magic against me. Beaten me relentlessly. Maybe I would be saving others from the same fate by speaking up. "The others were MacTavish and Bennett."

19

JAXON

I sat at the long boardroom table. Dean Wright had called a staff meeting now that the winter break was coming to an end. We'd been there for an hour going over the details for next term. My mind kept drifting to Caprice. Anger flared as I thought about what the Aimes kid had tried to do to her. I was grateful every minute of the day that we'd arrived in time. Though I still wished we'd shown up sooner.

Seeing her drunk and vulnerable had pierced my heart. I wanted nothing more than to take her home with me, to protect her forever. At least I had gotten to take her to my apartment, care for her, put her to bed. My pillow still faintly held her scent—sweet, floral.

Dean Wright stood, she held a paper with the Council seal on it. "I have some difficult news." Her gaze fell on me. "The Tromara have decided to punish Jaxon McIver for the crimes he committed in August. For intervening with the Tromara and Ms. Sorrentino."

I felt the blood leave my face. What would they demand of me? My life? I waited for her to continue.

"The Council has already agreed to their terms of punishment." She sucked in a deep breath, glancing at the paper. "They demand a first-quarter year culling. Six names will be drawn to satisfy this demand."

Everyone started talking at once.

"But we've never culled more than once a year!"

"They said they'd forgiven that crime."

"Leave it to the son of a traitor…"

I buried my face in my hands. I should have known they wouldn't forgive such a crime. My ribcage felt like it was being crushed by an invisible vice. I struggled to draw in a breath. Six people were going to die because of what I did. Six more, who had a chance to stay out of the Culling Club before this, would sink down to fill those empty spots.

May, Liam, and Angel all sent me pitying looks. Several of the others openly glared.

"Quiet down," Dean Wright called. "I want to get this over and done with. Remember we are preserving the Truce. The Truce is all that matters. It gives future generations a chance to live in peace. It allows the majority of us to keep our lives. Now Ms. Duinn will pull names from the—"

"No." I stood. "I'll do it."

"Jaxon, you don't need to punish yourself for—"

"They are being culled because of me. I will pull the names. It's my responsibility."

The dean studied me for several heartbeats, then nodded. "As you wish."

As a group, we walked down to the entry hall of the administration building. The billboard glowed with all of the first year's students names and their points ranking.

"The selection must be random," said the dean. "The board is already magiced to be unbiased." She glanced at me. "Whenever you're ready."

I withdrew my carnelian wand. With a flick, I sent the random selection spell that would only highlight six names below the ten percent line. The next moment all six turned from yellow to a deep red.

I couldn't suppress the sigh of relief that came. Caprice had not been chosen. She was safe.

Unfortunately, Aimes had not been selected either.

"It is done." Dean Wright turned to face us. "The culling shall be held in three days. You are all dismissed."

Several of my colleagues shot me more glares as they left the hall.

"Don't mind them," May said, standing next to me.

"They're right to look at me like that," I said in a low voice. "I should never have come to teach here." Not that I had a choice.

The hall emptied out except for the four of us. Liam and Angel wore matching expressions of concern. May rubbed my back in soothing circles, which I resisted the urge to shake off. I could go on a killing rampage and these three would find a way to take my side. I appreciated that, but it also made me angry.

"I need to call Isabella. She'll want to know if Caprice was selected or not." I took long strides to the stairs that led up to the building's staff turret. It had the best cell reception up there.

Taking my phone from my pocket, I pressed the button to dial Isabella's number. She answered on the first ring.

"She's safe," I said immediately.

Isabella sighed in relief. "I'm so sorry, Jaxon. There was nothing I could do. The Tromara left us no choice."

"I know. Don't worry about it." I didn't think I was doing a good job at convincing her. "It is what it is."

"You're so stoic. But I know you. And I'm sorry for this." She sighed again. "It will all be over soon."

"Yeah." It would all be over soon. Until the next time. Then we'd just tell ourselves that again: It will all be over soon. Round and round it went.

Not for the first time, I understood exactly why my father led that rebellion. But those were treasonous thoughts. We had to uphold the Truce for the greater good. For the ninety percent of supernaturals who lived safe lives because of the culling. That was what was right, and good. Sometimes it just didn't feel right or good.

The next two days were a blur of sorrow-filled activity. First the hate-mail started arriving in my mailbox. They were letters from the parents whose children would be culled too soon. I read every one of them, it was the least I could do for my crimes. Then I tucked them away in a drawer.

I would never make the mistake of going against the Tromara again.

The day after that, the parents started arriving to say farewell to their children. That day I spent hiding in my apartment. It was a cowardly act, but I couldn't face them. And they didn't want to see me either. These people all thought they had six more months together. They were cheated out of that time.

Lounging on the couch, I took another swig of bourbon from the bottle. Now half empty. They were cheated, and they held me account-able—which was fine. It was more than half my fault. But, I doubted the Tromara were getting hate-mail for their decision, or the Council for agreeing to this culling.

More treasonous thoughts. Maybe I was a bad seed after all—my father's son. Obviously my decisions were misguided. I was a hazard to the supernatural community. This proved it.

I took a long swallow. The burn down my throat wasn't as harsh anymore. In fact, it was starting to feel numb. Like the rest of me. I slumped deeper into the sofa, the bottle resting on my bare chest.

Someone pounded at my door.

"Go away!" The words came out strong and steady. Obviously, I needed to drink more.

A clicking sound reached me as the door unlocked. The handle turned.

"What the fuck—" I'd locked it. But Liam had the spare key. Damn. He had all the spare keys, in case any of us did anything stupid. That was his reasoning. What about him doing something stupid, he never mentioned that. Which of us was supposed to barge in on him when he didn't want it?

I glanced down at my boxers. No point in getting dressed if it was just the guys. I tilted my head to see the door. Big brown eyes in a pretty face peeked around the edge. I frowned. That wasn't the guys.

20

CAPRICE

I stepped into Jaxon's apartment. He was sprawled on one of the couches, wearing only boxers, with a bottle of booze in his hands. Tentatively, I closed the door behind me, knowing that May and Liam were out there if I needed them. Still, I wasn't sure this was a good idea.

"Jaxon? Are you okay?" I asked, approaching the sofa like it held a tiger rather than a depressed, inebriated man.

"What are you doing here? How'd you get in here?" His eyes were slightly glazed, but his voice held steady. It was hard to measure his level of intoxication.

I sat down on the sofa across from him. My gaze raking over his powerful thighs and sculpted chest. His hair was mussed in the most sexy way possible. He must look like this when he wakes up in the morning.

I refocused on his face, I had a purpose here. And it was not to lust after him. "Isabella told me what happened. May and Liam said you weren't doing too well."

"Nosy bastards." He lifted the bottle to his lips, his throat moved as he gulped. Dear God, he was really on the path to self-destruction.

"I think they just care about you," I offered, pulling the long sweater sleeves to cover my knuckles.

He narrowed his eyes at me. "What do you want?"

"To make you feel better."

His lips twisted with a wry smile as his gaze traveled to my lips, breasts, legs, and back up again. "I can think of a way to make me feel better."

Yeah... that proved it. He was trashed. Sober Jaxon would never be so obviously flirtatious. Unless he was trying to pump me for information. This man was still a riddle.

His grey eyes filled with heat. An answering response zipped through me, making my nipples grow hard. His smile transformed from mocking to knowing. I really was in the lion's den.

I dug my fingernails into my palms. The pain distracted me from thoughts of completely taking advantage of Jaxon in his vulnerable state. As hot and exciting as that would be, it wasn't a good idea. I wanted him sober the first time I took him. Where had that thought come from?

I cleared my throat. "I just came to say that this isn't your fault. It's mine. I'm the one who went out after dark. The Tromara found me. I was stupid—"

"I rescued you from them. So it's my fault."

"If I hadn't gone out, you wouldn't have had to rescue me. So it's my fault."

"Look here, cupcake, it's my fault. Because I say it is. Got it?"

I didn't think it was possible, but he was even more stubborn when he was drunk.

"Uh, no. You can't just bully me into believing that. It was my fault and we both know it."

He grunted. "You're too damned stubborn."

"That's the pot calling the kettle—"

"I thought you were supposed to be making me feel better." He sulked.

"I was—I am. You don't make it easy."

"You could try harder." That wry grin reappeared.

I sighed. "Obviously, you're beyond my help." I stood, walking past him to reach the door.

His hand shot out and caught my wrist. "Don't leave me," he whispered, his eyes closing. "Please."

I stilled. He drew me closer, until I was sitting at the edge of the couch, my hip pressed against his stomach. He set the bottle down on the coffee table, then caressed my face with both hands. With a gentle tug, he pulled me down until my lips met his.

His kiss was light, his tongue brushed across my lips, as if asking for permission. My lips parted and I pressed deeper into him. His tongue entered my mouth, caressing, exploring. I didn't even care that his hot breath was laced with bourbon. Every fiber in me wanted him. Wanted to drink him in.

In a rare moment of clarity, I pushed away. "You're drunk. And you're my teacher. You're going to regret this. Liam and May are right outside."

"I'm not that drunk." Then he hollered, "You two can leave now, I'm in good hands." He pulled me in for another scorching kiss. "I'm your teacher and your advisor, but that doesn't matter here. Of course, I won't do anything you don't want me to do."

Was there anything that I *didn't* want him to do? The dragon-shifter in me was stirring. Tempting me to give in completely and just enjoy myself. No regrets, no consequences. More than that, the dragon wanted to claim him. To make him mine. Like a treasure.

Jaxon held my face in his hands, studying me. "I could use a distraction right now. I want to explore you, just a little, and feel you come in my hands. Would you like that?" His voice was gruff.

I nodded, my heart leaping against my ribs.

"Good." He claimed my mouth in another searing kiss. Then he rolled us off the couch, and onto the plush rug. He straddled my leg, his cock leaving a hot imprint against my hip. With one swift motion he had my sweater up and off over my head. He groaned, burying his face in my cleavage. "You're so damned beautiful." With another expert move, he unhooked my bra and tossed it aside.

Jaxon gently squeezed one breast then the other. His thumb circled my nipple. I gasped, my back arching off the floor. With a confident male grin, he brought his mouth down, his tongue teased my flesh.

I closed my eyes and moaned. When he was finished with one nipple, he repeated the tongue strokes on the other one. His hand slid down to caress my stomach. He unbuttoned my jeans, slipping his hand inside my panties.

His fingers stroked my hot, wet flesh. He spread my legs wider with his thigh. When he found my clit, I gasped. I'd never been touched by a man like this before. My first time had been brief straight-forward intercourse with a clueless teenager. Nothing like this. Heat and tingles sparked all over my body.

He rhythmically stroked that sensitive nub, as his mouth claimed mine again. I moaned into him. He increased the pressure and pace with his fingers. My breath was coming in ragged gasps. He moved his lips to my jaw, neck, collarbone. Everywhere he kissed lit my skin on fire.

The pressure in me was building, I felt like I was going to explode into a million pieces. He took my nipple into his mouth again. I shattered. He groaned, nipping at the soft underside of my breast.

I shuddered once more, all tension leaving my body.

His hands slid up to palm both my breasts. "Fuck, that was hot."

"Mmmm." It was the most coherent sound I could make.

Jaxon beamed down at me. He kissed the tip of my nose. "I hope you liked that, cupcake." He rolled over onto his back, then settled my head against his chest. A strong arm wrapped around my waist.

"What about you? I can..." My fingers trailed down his stomach toward the tent in his boxers. He caught my hand, bringing it to his lips for a kiss.

"Not today. Just relax."

The entire school stood in the chilly night air. Waiting.

At the south-western corner of campus, hidden in the trees, was the Culling Arena. The structure was reminiscent of the old Roman fighting pits. Stadium seating rose in a semi-circle around the large, empty space in the middle. At the far side stood the Culling Gate that would open to the woods beyond when the time was right.

I shivered, hugging my coat closer. Jaxon and May sat on either side of me, their expressions schooled to hide emotion.

Jaxon reached over to take my hand in his. I wasn't sure if it was to comfort me or him. Perhaps both, since we both felt guilty over what was about to happen. This was our mistake, and my fellow students were going to be prematurely offered up to the Tromara because of it.

I shuddered. Jaxon squeezed my hand. Seated beside him were Liam and Angel. Liam's face wore a deep frown. I wouldn't want to be him right then, feeling everyone's emotions. That would be overwhelming. It must suck to be a fae at times.

Angel's usually intense eyes were dull—distant. Like he was mentally checked out of the situation. I wished I had that capability.

A door to one side of the stadium creaked open. Six students were shoved into the open space by three large men I'd never seen before. I swallowed hard. Several of the sullen faces I recognized from the Culling Club party. One in particular I recognized from History class— the goth vampire girl.

Like the other five, she was dressed in a long black robe that cinched at the waist. Her feisty, tough-girl persona had vanished. Already she seemed like a shell of her former self, as her sad eyes scanned the audience who would witness her sacrifice.

Dean Wright held a loudspeaker in her hand as she addressed us. "We offer this sacrifice to the Tromara to preserve the Truce. The Truce is a blessing for us. Given to us by the gracious generosity of the

Tromara. We are grateful for the peace in our lives because of this agreement, and we will always strive to uphold it."

The three men who'd ushered the students out, retreated back through the side door. A moment later, the Culling Gate began to slide open. It creaked and groaned, usually only being opened once a year.

A cold sweat broke over my skin. Beasts, like the big, nasty vampire who smelled of blood and death, the one who'd attacked me, were coming for them. Yet, none of the students cried out or tried to escape. They stood in the middle of the arena, staring beyond the gate. Were they drugged? No one could face death, or worse, that stoically. Could they?

Once the gate had fully opened, ten forms in long trench coats strode in. The area was lit well enough to see their greasy hair and feral eyes. They weren't humans or supernaturals. They were monsters. I instinctively leaned closer to Jaxon.

The large vampire who'd attacked me in Isabella's garden was among them. His gaze scanned the audience until he found me. His eyes locked with mine, like a promise that he would finish what he'd started a few months ago.

Five of the students were hauled over the Tromara's shoulders and taken away. The last one, the vampire girl, was approached by my attacker. She whimpered as he took her face in his beefy hands. He tilted her head to the side, bared his teeth, and ripped open her neck.

She screamed as the pain cut through whatever drug had rendered her docile. Blood flowed to the packed-dirt floor. He held onto her, feeding as she weakly struggled.

I stared in horror. My body rigid, stuck in place as I watched the Tromara vampire drain my schoolmate. Her body slumped, and he let her slide to the ground. Two other Tromara, who'd been watching, lifted her corpse between them and walked out into the woods.

With one last glance at me, the vampire followed them out.

I sat petrified. My gaze fixed on that pool of blood as the gate noisily slid shut. They'd taken her body. Were they going to eat her flesh next? They were cannibals.

How could this be okay? I glanced around the arena at the other students and faculty members. Several were crying, but most had taken the experience in stride as if it were a normal occurrence. This was normal to them. I couldn't wrap my brain around that.

I knew the history. I knew about the wars, the dwindling supernatural numbers, and the forming of the Truce. But this couldn't be the answer for a peaceful existence. This was bullshit!

Anger warmed my insides. I pushed it down. Even now, I couldn't get angry or bad things might happen. I felt like I was going to explode with rage at my own helplessness.

I caught Liam studying me. He knew how I felt. I was sure he could correctly guess why too. I clenched my jaw, wanting to scream, and cry, and rain down destruction on the Tromara. Though the supernaturals were also to blame. They'd agreed to this, accepted it, and embraced it. I wanted to slap the shit out of them!

I pulled my hand free from Jaxon's. He was one of them. He accepted this world and the terms that went with it. Was I the only one who thought the Truce should go to hell?

Jaxon frowned down at me, but didn't say anything. Surely, my anger showed clearly on my face.

"I need to get back to my room." I stood, shoving past everyone in that row. Jaxon followed. He insisted on having someone with me at all times. Aimes was still in the hospital, but MacTavish and Bennett were wandering free—for now.

We strode in silence to my door. Jaxon caught my shoulder and turned me to face him.

"I'm sorry," he said.

I bet he was. They were all sorry. But no one had the guts to speak up and change anything. I nodded curtly.

He brushed his lips against mine. When I didn't kiss him back, he straightened, stepping back. His gaze searched my eyes, then dropped to the floor. "I'll see you later."

I let myself into the room. Madison hadn't returned yet, which I was grateful for. I needed space, and time to myself. Six people had just lost their lives—whether they were dead or slaves to the Tromara, it amounted to the same thing. Six students would now sink into the Culling Club to take their places. This was my fault.

Whether it was burning down my foster families home, or getting six innocent people killed, I was a walking disaster. Even Jaxon wouldn't be in trouble, and feeling horrible about himself, if I'd never come into his life.

I had to leave. I had to get as far away from the supernatural community as possible. So far, my dragon-shifter abilities included collecting seashells and seducing hot men. I could totally blend into the human world. No one would need to know that I was different. I could go to college with Elena...except the Tromara would probably hunt me down. I had to go far away. To Europe.

My gut twisted. Would the Tromara kill Isabella if I left, even if she didn't help me leave? Could they take out the queen? If I left, it would also open up a spot in the Culling Club. One more death would be on my head.

I sank down to the edge of my bed. This was hopeless. *Everything* was hopeless.

21

CAPRICE

Two nights later, Liam knocked on my door. My mood hadn't improved, so I narrowed my eyes up at him. "What do you want?"

He steadily held my gaze. "May wants to see you in her office."

I didn't want to see anybody else, but I couldn't refuse May. She'd been nothing but kind to me. I grunted, stepping into the hall. "Fine."

We walked side by side across the lawn. All the students had returned from their holiday break to witness the culling, and since the new term started after the weekend, most had decided to stay on campus. The place no longer resembled a ghost town.

"I can tell something's eating away at you. What is it?" Liam asked.

"You can't guess?" Maybe I'd overestimated his emotion-reading abilities. And his intellectual level.

"The culling of course. I know you blame yourself. Is there anything else bothering you? That's what I was asking." His shoulder brushed mine. He quickly jerked away, but I caught the movement.

"That's it. There's nothing else on my mind."

"You're angry at me. Why?"

I sighed. "I'm not angry at you. I'm annoyed at all your emotion prodding. Just leave me alone. I'm fine." I sped up the pathway.

"Yeah, you seem fine," Liam said under his breath.

I twisted my head around to glare at him.

We stepped into May's office. She was chatting with another woman, who I didn't recognize.

"There you two are," May said, coming to greet me. "Caprice, this is Nalea."

I shook the woman's hand, admiring her black mane of super curly hair.

"Nalea is one of the shifter teachers," May continued.

"Oh?" I glanced at her with more interest.

"I'm a lion-shifter. May thought I might be able to help you." Nalea's smile warmed her deep brown and gold eyes.

May trained her gaze on me. "Have you figured out how to let that inner shifter out? Any progress over the past two weeks?"

"Uh, no, not really." Too much other crazy stuff had happened, that I'd nearly forgotten I was supposed to be working on unblocking my abilities.

"That's okay," May said. "I've arranged for Nalea to give you private instruction at the start of term. You'll train with her after your classes three days a week."

"So the dean still hasn't approved me for shifter classes?"

May's face fell. "No. You're enrolled in witch classes again. But only until you can prove you're a shifter."

My heart sank. More witch classes. More failure.

"Thanks, May, for doing all of this." I didn't want her to think I was ungrateful. She'd been trying too hard to help me.

"Of course." She hugged me. "Your new class schedule should be arriving later tonight. I'll see you on Monday."

I followed Liam out of the office.

"You know, I can help you with the mental blocks. If those are keeping you abilities locked up." He sounded like he genuinely wanted to.

"No offense, but I don't want you poking around inside my head."

"Even if it could save your life? Get you out of the Culling Club?" His brow creased in confusion.

I sighed. "My privacy is more important to me at this point."

"Is this because of you and Jaxon?"

"Partly."

Liam was quiet for several seconds. "Jaxon is a good man. I'm happy for you both."

"We're not like officially together or anything. It was just that one time..."

"Really?" He frowned. "Well, you might want to clear that up with him then."

"What? Why?"

"Let's just say your relationship is a little more solidified in his mind."

I blushed. "Oh. Good to know." I hadn't seen Jaxon since the culling. My gut clenched, I hoped he was doing okay. Having sunk into my own depression, I hadn't considered that he must be feeling equally as horrible. I should go see him. Or maybe I shouldn't. I didn't know what I was doing any more. About anything.

I watched Liam out of the corner of my eye. Those full lips still made my stomach flutter. Part of me was hoping I had a class with him next term, so that I could listen to his voice for an hour and daydream about naughty things. It would be a delightful distraction.

I still couldn't believe I was feeling like getting this intimate with my teachers. After what Jaxon and I had done in his apartment, I was surprised that I didn't feel weirder about it. Maybe I wouldn't feel too weird about kissing Liam either.

How could I feel this way toward both him and Jaxon at the same time?

The whole dragon-shifter and multiple mates thing still freaked me out. That was fun in theory. But how could it work in the real world? People were innately jealous, right?

I figured I should prove that they were. In a particularly dark spot along the pathway, I gripped Liam's bicep to stop him. "Are you jealous? Of Jaxon?"

His eyes widened. "No. Of course not. I mean, besides that one kiss, nothing has ever happened between us. I have no claim on you. But you and Jaxon—"

I pulled his face down, capturing his lips with mine. He froze for an instant. Then he kissed me back. Urgently. His tongue plunged into my mouth, seeking and caressing. For all of his gentleness in voice and manner, he was a savage kisser.

His lean, muscled arms wrapped around my waist, pulling my body fully against his. One hand moved down to palm my butt, then held me in place as he rocked his erection against my pelvis. Heat coursed through me. I moaned into his mouth.

I *could* feel this way about two men at the same time. I craved everything he had to offer. But I wanted the same from Jaxon. They were so different from each other, unique. And I wanted it all.

Liam broke his lips away from mine. "I can't do this." His voice was rough, tight.

"Because of Jaxon?"

"No. For other reasons. I can't." His hands gripped my waist, setting me arms length away from him. His chest rose and fell rapidly. I could tell he wanted me as much as I wanted him. But for some reason he was holding back.

"Do you think I'm a horrible slut?" My heart was still racing from his kisses.

He squeezed his eyes shut for a moment. "No. May told us about dragon-shifters. She wanted to give us a heads up. I've come to terms with your nature."

I didn't believe that for a second. "Then why?"

"I can't tell you exactly why. All I can say, is it's because of my father."

"Oh." I didn't push for more. "I'm sorry."

His lips twisted into a sad smile. " So am I." He wrapped my hand around his arm. "Let's get you back to your dorm."

Because of the end of term culling, New Year's was a depressing non-event. No one felt like celebrating. The holiday decorations disappeared over night. Then a day later, I received my schedule for the new term.

11:00pm - 11:55pm - Math - Gi Hall Rm 202

12:15am - 1:10am - Magic 102 - Aeras Hall Rm 100

Break

2:00am - 2:55am - Magical Ethics - Gi Hall Rm 317

3:15am - 4:10am - Potions 2 - Gi Hall Rm 201

Private Tutoring (M,W,F) - TBD

Dinner

All I saw in this was pass, fail, probably fail, fail, and probably fail. Today was Saturday and classes started on Monday. Not a lot of time to come up with a game plan.

I had to get out of there. The supernatural world was fucking insane. I couldn't stop the Tromara from taking whoever they wanted. I couldn't help anyone. Not even myself.

The deadly promise in that Tromara vampire's eyes haunted my dreams and waking hours alike. No happily ever after was coming for me. Only slavery, endless fear, and probably an untimely death.

I wanted to believe those monsters wouldn't hurt Isabella when I disappeared, so I convinced myself that it was true. My chest seized. This was a selfish decision. But I was going to go through with it anyway. I had to. I should have left sooner.

The Tromara had received their sacrifices just days ago, so hopefully they'd gone back to wherever they lived. I'd sneak out at dawn, which was only six hours away. Then I'd run as far as I could, hitchhike into Portland, and call my old foster parents Antonio and Vanessa. Luckily, I still had my phone checked-out from the dean's office. During the winter break, they'd been more lax about letting us keep our devices, but only until tomorrow night.

I emptied my backpack of school books and started filling it with a change of clothes, my seashell collection, the gifts from Isabella, toiletries, and food from the common room. I dressed in warm layers, pulling on a pair of hiking boots that I rarely wore. I stowed my pack under my bed for later.

Thankfully, Madison had been spending less time in our room since I'd been moping about. She wouldn't be back until close to dawn. I had several hours to kill before implementing the next phase of my plan. If I was going to be up all day, I should get some rest.

I managed to doze on and off for a few hours, fully clothed under my blankets. Near dawn, Madison came in, humming softly. She lazily changed into her pajamas, then settled into bed. I waited for her soft snoring to fill the room.

Quickly, I reached under the bed and grabbed my pack. I crept across the room, avoiding the squeaky floorboards. Slowly opening the bedroom door, I peered into the quiet hall.

Madison mumbled in her sleep and turned over. I froze, until she'd settled, then slipped into the hallway. Most people were asleep at this hour. The hall was empty, as was the common room downstairs.

Outside, the overcast sky was growing lighter in the east. I decided the best route out was the gate closest to me, behind Sorrentino Hall. It was also the furthest from the Culling Gate.

I approached it, surveying the high iron bars that joined the stone wall on either side. A thick steal chain secured the closure. Even bolt cutters would have a hard time biting through that. Climbing over it seemed like the only option. I eyed the spikes at the top. Lovely.

Taking a few steps back, I glanced at the stone wall instead. No trees grew close enough to it to climb and make it over. The stone itself was smooth, unclimbable. So the gate it would have to be.

I managed to get my backpack through the bars. It squeezed through after several full-body shoves. I tried to get my head and shoulders through, just in case it would work, but it didn't.

I launched myself at the iron gate, scurrying up the bars. Luckily, there were crossbars at somewhat reasonable intervals. Keeping people out—or in—was the job of the spikes at the top. As I neared them, I began to doubt the wisdom of my decision. They were three foot long impaling instruments.

Clinging near the top of the gate, I evaluated my options. Either get back down and find another way, give up completely, grow wings, or somehow slide my ass through these things. There was a high chance that I'd get stuck trying to slide through. But it was better than all the other options.

I shimmied up, squeezing first my head, then my torso through the spikes where they were most open—at the top. I held onto the sharp edges, lifting myself from one side of the gate to the other. Carefully, and slowly. Then I started to descend.

The last few feet, I let go, dropping to the ground. I snatched up my pack and swung it over my shoulders. It was going to be a long hike out of here. The day looked like it was going to bring more rain.

I set off through the trees, forging my own path. The forest was eerily quiet even for winter. Every fallen branch that cracked under my boots sounded too loud. In no time, the rainwater from the ferns had soaked through my jeans.

Portland was west and north from the Academy. Which meant I needed to skirt around the school. For the first half hour I walked east, just to get some distance. Then I turned northward. Eventually, I'd have to run into something. A road. A town. Anything.

I rounded a patch of close growing pines, coming face-to-face with a deer. "Whoa!" It ran off. I wasn't sure which of us was more startled.

The dark grey sky obscured the sun. Within an hour, I wasn't sure which direction I was going anymore. There were no straight pathways through the forest. I leaped over streams and fallen trees. Avoided thickets of brambles and slick embankments, it was slow going.

I tried to bring up a compass app on phone, but there was no service. For the first time, I wished I was one of those people who could make one out of a clock face, or a hairpin in a pool of water, or whatever.

A black blur caught my eye. I jerked my head toward it, but it had disappeared. My heart leaped into my throat. Was I seeing things? It was daytime, surely the Tromara wouldn't be out here. I knew that creepy vampire couldn't be.

I continued picking my way through the foreign landscape. Every small sound startled me. A bird taking flight from a tree branch. A squirrel scurrying down the side of a leafless maple. My nerves were on edge, my pulse too fast. I needed to get a grip.

The gentle pattering of rain suddenly turned violent. Huge drops pelted the top of my head and the surrounding ferns. I yelped, seeking shelter close to a large cedar, as the deluge intensified. The sound of rain was so loud, it filled my ears.

The deep grey sky lit up with a white flash. Thunder rolled, cracking overhead a second later. I cringed against the tree trunk.

A bolt of lightening narrowly missed the side of my head. What the hell? I glanced around the woods, my gaze snapping to the two duster-wearing figures who approached. They were both large men with shoulder-length hair and black eyes. Cruel eyes. I knew at once they were Tromara.

22

CAPRICE

The two Tromara witches pointed their wands at me. As one swished his, another bolt of lightning struck the tree behind me. I yelped, ducking while sliding around to the other side of the massive trunk. Then I ran. Rain stung my eyes as I tried to shield my face against it. Glancing back, the Tromara gave chase. They were more familiar with the terrain, easily navigating the underbrush and logs.

I pumped my legs harder. My throat burned from drawing in cold, rapid breaths. I couldn't let them catch me. I'd risked everything to get away from them. This couldn't be my fate.

A fallen tree lay in my path. I leaped over it, landing hard on the other side. My foot caught in a hole and yanked me to a stop. I fell forward, breaking my fall with my forearms. Quickly, I scrambled up to keep running.

Shouts reached me through the thunder of rainfall. I turned my head toward the noise. My breath hitched. Jaxon dueled with one of the Tromara witches, trading spells in rapid succession. Angel was in his large, black wolf form. He mauled the other witch who squirmed on the ground. Liam hovered to the side, his brilliant red-gold wings fluttering.

I was about to keep running away when three more Tromara came up behind Liam.

"Look out!" I shouted, too late.

They tackled Liam. One transformed into a grey wolf, his gaze trained on Angel. Jaxon was still focused on the witch he fought—neither of them seemed to be able to get the upper hand in the duel.

Instinct took over and I reversed direction. I had no plan. But I couldn't let them die for me.

I raced toward Liam. Two Tromara repeatedly kicked him in the stomach. One pulled a massive sword from the sheath on his back. He stood to the side, aiming the weapon at Liam's neck. He lifted the sword high, ready to bring it down on my sweet, bloodied fae.

Still several feet away from them, I wasn't going to arrive in time.

I screamed, yelling, "No!" With the word, a channel of flame burst from my throat. It scorched the Tromara's back, setting fire to his trench coat. He shrieked in pain and surprise. The other Tromara's eyes widened.

I reached Liam's side, skidding to a halt.

"He's mine! Back off," I roared at the monsters.

I rounded on the two still standing over us. The one who'd been on fire, had shrugged out of his flaming coat. He glared at me, raising his sword. I snarled. Another blaze of fire erupted from my mouth. They both wailed, going down in flame.

Adrenaline pumped through my veins. My senses heightened, tuning into the battle around me. The two wolves growled as they tore at each other. They were closest to me. I rushed the black one, spewing more fire. It yelped and backed off, running into the forest.

Freed from that fight, Angel focused on the witch who engaged Jaxon. He leaped on the Tromara's back, his canine jaw ripping open the witch's throat. The last Tromara fell to his knees, then face-planted in a puddle of his own blood.

I breathed hard, searching the area for more signs of threat. Liam had regained his feet. He and the other two stared at me, not bothering to hide their expressions, which ranged from shocked to curious.

I glanced down at my hands. Black scales covered my skin. It felt like they covered my entire body. My clothes brushed roughly against the scales, making all of my skin feel prickly. Long black nails tipped my fingers.

I blinked. I'd finally done it. Finally morphed into a dragon-shifter. I'd breathed *fire*. Holy shit!

With a glance at the guys, I opened my mouth to say something, but nothing came out. I was at a loss for words. I tried again. "Are you all right?"

That seemed to awaken them from their collective trance.

Jaxon's steely eyes filled with anger. "We need to leave. Now. Before more of those monsters come for us." With his hand, he made a throwing gesture at the ground near Liam. The fae vanished in a haze of purple smoke. Jaxon repeated the process for Angel. Then he approached me. "I have some choice words for you!" He took my waist, slamming me forcefully against his chest. His mouth captured mine—hard, desperate. I felt all of his rage and fear in that kiss. Without easing up, he threw the spell at the ground and the purple smoke teleported us.

I sat on a couch sipping coffee next to Liam. Jaxon and Angel sat across from us, their arms folded over their chests. No one had uttered a word in several long minutes. I got it, they were mad at me—livid. Giving me the silent treatment. I wouldn't blame any of them if they never wanted to talk to me again.

I stared at the coffee table, unwilling to meet the fury in Jaxon's eyes. I'd totally fucked up. I'd put them in danger. Myself in danger.

Possibly Isabella, too. Hell, maybe even the whole supernatural community.

We'd killed four of the five Tromara who'd attacked us. I doubted the cannibals were just going to let that slide. I'd burned two of them to death, for fuck's sake.

I dared to take a quick peek at the guys. All of their faces were set with hard lines—even Liam's. They'd come to my rescue, knowing full well that the Tromara would take their lives for it. Why? They should have just left me to my fate. Anger flared in me. They were self-sacrificing bastards!

I bit my tongue. I wanted to do was rip into them, but I knew that wasn't fair. My anger stemmed from that fact that I cared about these three men, and I was completely helpless to make sure they were safe. Shame washed over me.

I broke the silence with a soft, "I'm sorry."

"You'd goddamned better be!" Jaxon roared. "Do you have any idea what this means for us?"

"You should have thought of that before you came after me!" My chest clenched. If only he hadn't played the hero. I'd made a stupid decision and deserved to face the consequences alone.

"I did. Believe me, I tried to talk myself out of it, Caprice." His eyes flashed.

"Then why did you do it?"

"Because I don't want to live without you!" His tone was enraged, but the words threw me off balance.

I blinked at him. "Wh-what?"

Jaxon ran a hand through his tousled blond waves. "Never mind." He stood up, walking to the kitchen.

My gaze trailed after him. He didn't want to live without me? Was he in love with me? Was I with him? My chest filled with an unfamiliar sensation.

I glanced at the other two. Angel stared hard at the floor. Liam said,

"We're all in this together now. Whatever the Tromara decide for punishment, we'll each take our part of it."

His resigned tone melted my heart. They'd each decided to sacrifice themselves for me. Jaxon had just told me why he'd done it. Angel and Liam must have reasons too, even if I didn't know what they were.

"I'm so sorry, guys. I screwed up big time. This is all my fault." I swallowed hard. "Let me take the punishment—"

"Not going to happen," Jaxon called from the other room.

"Caprice, stop," Liam said.

Angel shook his head.

I was outnumbered. Going up against them, I was beginning to learn, was futile. They were each as stubborn as me, if not more so. I glanced at Jaxon's back as he stood over the sink. I wished I could see his face, read what he was thinking.

I wished I knew what they were all thinking, and feeling. Had Liam and Angel risked their lives for me, or for Jaxon? Either way this was my fault.

"Are you angry with me too?" I asked May as I closed the door to her office.

She pursed her lips. "Not angry. Disappointed."

"You're *disappointed*? Your brother could lose his life because of me!"

"He makes his own choices." She waved away my concerns.

I sighed, then stifled a yawn. I'd been up for too many hours, but May wanted to see me before I went to bed. So here I was.

Her eyes lit with excitement. "You shifted. I want you to do it again."

"Right now? Here?"

"Yes. While the sensation is still fresh in your mind. Give it a go." She was relentless.

I closed my eyes, remembering back a few hours to when I'd morphed. Heat crept over my skin, sending prickly sensations through me.

May gasped.

I opened my eyes. I'd done it again. My hands were covered in those black scales with the reddish glow. I touched my face, feeling the same scaly texture there.

"What do I look like?" I asked her.

She snapped her mouth shut, retrieving a mirror from a drawer. "Take a look." She held it in front of my face.

"Holy fuck!" I ducked away from it. That wasn't me, that was a *monster*.

"Mmm. Yeah, that might take a moment to sink in. Take it slow." May placed the mirror in my hands.

Slowly, I brought it up, summoning up the courage for a quick peek. I didn't have a snout or anything, but my face was covered in scales. My pupils were slit like a snakes. The irises glowed a red-orange. If I'd had snakes for hair, I'd look like Medusa. Thankfully, my long black mane was the same as always.

"Well, what do you think?" May asked, leaning against her desk.

How was she not terrified of me? "This will take some getting used to."

"Yeah, but it's...wow. You breathe fire too?"

"I'm not doing that here."

"That's fine. But you can, right?" Her eyes shone with excitement.

I nodded.

Suddenly a memory, fully formed and vivid, came crashing into my mind.

I was in a dark room with dirty carpet. The shouting reached me from downstairs, and fear pinched my chest. I ran to the stairs at the end of the hall. From below my foster father's voice boomed, "Clumsy bitch, she deserves the belt!"

I glanced down to the living room, where my six-year-old foster sister stood crying. Her glass of orange juice all over the carpet. My foster mother cowered against the wall, her voice placating. "She's just a child."

My foster father undid his leather belt, folding it in half. He reached for the little girl. I sprinted into the room and shoved her behind me. Shielding her small frame with my larger, teenaged one.

"Get out of the way, Caprice!" He roared. "Or you'll get some of this too."

"I won't let you hurt her." I was furious. I'd had enough by that point.

He lunged at me, trying to get to the girl I protected.

"No!" I screamed, cringing away. With the words came a channel of flame. It narrowly missed him, instead lighting the carpet and drapes on fire.

He jerked back, wide-eyed and pale. I stared at the raging inferno as it spread in the room. Gathering my wits, I grabbed my foster sister and ran for the front door.

May tugged at my arm. "Caprice? Are you okay?"

I blinked a few times, coming back to the present. I'd suppressed that memory. It had been so deeply buried in my subconscious that it only came out in snippets through my dreams. A wave of dizziness swept through me.

"I need to sit down." I sank into a chair. "I remember what happened. The traumatic event that caused me to suppress my abilities. I *did* burn that house down."

May made a sympathetic face. "Do you want to tell me about it?"

I nodded, then launched into the whole story.

Dean Wright suspended me from all activities, including classes. She'd decide what to do with me once she heard from the Council. Jaxon,

Liam, and Angel were also put on house arrest. Several of the other teachers took over their classes.

Madison pretty much ignored me as she came and went. I may as well have already been dead—I was to her. So I spent my days reading, and occasionally playing with my dragon-shifter abilities. I was getting used to the red-orange eyes and scales. They felt natural, like a normal part of me.

We didn't have to wait long for news. Although it did't come by way of the Council as everyone had expected.

The din of a hundred conversations penetrated my dorm window. Glancing out, it seemed the entire student body milled around on the lawn. The teachers strode toward the Dean's Hall.

I opened the window, leaning out. "What's going on?"

A witch from last term's potions class answered. "The Tromaraking is here. All the teachers have been called in by Dean Wright."

My stomach sank. They were here from me. To determine my punishment. And that of the guys, too.

"I didn't know the Tromara had a king." I called down.

The witch's eyes filled with fear. "No one's seen him since the last rebellion."

Yet, he'd shown up tonight. To deal with me and the guys for killing his men. Which basically meant we were in deep shit.

23

LIAM

The Tromara's leader, King Sebastian Anastos, was difficult to read, like he had a veil shielding his emotions. Or maybe he didn't have any emotions. Either way, I couldn't get a read on him. He appeared vampire, with pale skin under long, wavy black hair. His fangs showed when he spoke. Those dark eyes gave away nothing, but my senses told me there was something more to him.

I stood with the rest of the Academy faculty at one end of the large room, while the other was occupied by nearly twenty Tromara—the most I'd ever seen gathered in one place. They were of course there to protect their king. Each was more sinister looking than the last—all large men with dead eyes. Who knew what they hid under those trench coats. Not that it mattered, they were all deadly, even without weapons.

"You have confirmed that this girl is in fact a dragon-shifter? From the legends of old?" King Sebastian asked.

Dean Wright's face was pale, but her voice came out steady enough. "We have, Your Grace."

A hint of annoyance flickered across the Tromaraking's face. I had the distinct impression that he was disappointed that she'd offered up the truth so easily. He'd wanted her to lie. But one of his creatures had seen Caprice in her dragon form. We'd made sure to tell the dean every detail before this audience with the Tromara. Was he trying to catch us in a lie and lay a trap?

"Is she comely?" he asked.

Dean Wright startled. "I beg your pardon, Your Grace?"

"The girl. Is she attractive?" he asked, his voice filling the cavernous room.

A chill zipped across my scalp. There was no reason for him to ask a question like that, unless...

"Of course. All supernaturals are attractive, Your Grace." Dean Wright was pushing it with such a flippant comment.

The king sneered. "Some more so than others."

The dean inclined her head.

"She is a Sorrentino." It wasn't a question, he knew. "She would be the next queen." His dark gaze roved over each of us. "Killing three of my men is an unforgivable offense and puts the Truce on precarious ground. However..." he paused, "I have decided on the penalty for your crimes. The Truce will stand, and your kind will continue to be protected under it. In exchange for this Sorrentino girl. Either through the culling or when she graduates, this future Council Queen will be my bride."

My stomach dropped. Standing next to me, Angel growled. The low, threatening rumble drawing attention.

King Sebastian pinned the two of us, then Jaxon, with his dark gaze. "You are the three guilty ones. The ones who love her." He looked us over, the sneer returning to his lips. "This punishment is for each of you."

I clenched my jaw tight under his scrutiny. How did he know what we were feeling? Only fae had that ability among supernaturals. Or was he simply assuming since we risked our lives for her that we loved her?

He continued, "What do you think of that? Of her as my wife?" His gaze flitted to Jaxon. "I'm going to pound into her until she screams my name. I'll take her over and—"

Angel lunged at the Tromaraking, morphing into wolf-form midair. His jaw opened wide, as he focused for his attack to land on the vampire's neck.

Time seemed to slow down. The faculty members collectively gasped. Dean Wright's eyes widened in horror. Angel was going to get us all killed.

The Tromara leader didn't even flinch. In a fluid, graceful motion he flicked one hand at Angel, seconds before the wolf would have plowed into him. A bolt of red light left the Tromara's fingers, hitting Angel in the face. He dropped to the floor with a yelp, laying motionless on the smooth stone.

My body jerked in surprise. I took a step toward Angel.

"Stay where you are!" King Sebastian shouted. His gaze darted between me and Jaxon, whose face burned with fury.

The enemy's soldiers tensed, but didn't rush forward to protect their king. They waited, watching for his command and any other danger.

When their leader spoke to the dean, his voice was low. "Tell the Supernatural Council of my decision." His attention returned to me and Jaxon. "And you two, keep your hands off my bride-to-be." He gazed down at Angel's nude, human form. "Make sure to tell him that too."

The king turned on his heel, his soldiers closing in around him as they left.

Jaxon and I rushed to Angel. I found his steady pulse within seconds. Air whooshed from my lungs in relief. He was unconscious, but alive.

Dean Wright approached. "The moment he's recovered, send him to my office." Anger and fear rolled off her in nauseating waves. She stormed out of the hall. The other teachers followed, except May, who stood nearby hugging herself.

I went to her, wrapping an arm around her shoulders. She buried her face in my chest. We took comfort in each other's familiarity. Our heart rates gradually returning to normal.

Jaxon hadn't moved from where he crouched beside Angel. His emotions punched to my very core, resonating with my own: Rage, fear, and hopelessness.

The three of us paced or perched awkwardly around Jaxon's apartment, waiting for Angel to return from the dean's office. I sat on the arm of the couch facing the door, the Tromaraking's words replaying in my mind.

He'd baited us. He knew exactly what he was doing as he spoke and somehow read our emotions. Because of Angel's attack, he managed to show us how much more powerful he was than us. How going up against him was futile.

"He used magic," I muttered for the umpteenth time.

Jaxon halted his pacing long enough to throw me an exasperated glance.

"I know," May said from where she leaned against the kitchen counter. "I don't understand. He's a vampire. Vampires can't cast spells."

"They can't read emotions either." I rubbed a hand over my mouth. "It's impossible. All of it."

The door opened, and Angel stepped through with a sullen expression. "Hey, man," he said to me.

"How'd it go?" I asked, leaning forward.

Angel plopped down on the opposite couch. "You know. She ripped me a new one. If she could punish me, I'm sure she'd give me life in prison. But since the Tromara let it go, she has to as well."

"Why'd you attack him?" Jaxon asked, his features rigid.

Angel shrugged. "Fucker pissed me off." He brushed off Jaxon's question. "Now what the fuck are we going to do about Caprice?"

Jaxon grunted, but didn't get on Angel's case.

"What can we do?" May asked.

I twisted around to face her. "That *we*, it doesn't include you. Actually, I think you should leave."

May crossed her arms and huffed. "I'm part of this all too."

"No you're not." I stared her down. "The three of us are in trouble. Not you. You haven't done anything wrong and I want to keep it that way."

"You can't boss me around, little brother."

I stood, towering over her by several inches. "Really? You're going to pull that card?"

"Enough!" Jaxon grabbed May's arm, hauling her toward the door. "He's right. You're out of here."

May dug her heals into the carpet. "You can't—"

"It's my apartment, so I can." He opened the door, pushed her through, and waved his wand in a spell that turned the deadbolt, probably casting a warding charm with it. He strode over to the couches, taking a seat next to Angel, the two of them facing me. "Any one have any brilliant ideas?"

"One of us should tell Caprice," I said.

Jaxon's jaw worked. "Tell her what? *The fucking Tromaraking is going to force you to marry him and there's nothing we can do about it?* That'll go over well."

Angel sighed. "Besides starting another war, there is nothing we can do about it."

"Maybe it's time," Jaxon said under his breath.

I felt a surge of determination in Jaxon's emotions. He was serious. He'd start a war over a woman. Unbelievable. Who was I kidding? I'd do it too, for Caprice. Angel probably would, as well. The Tromara's leader had said his decision was to punish the three of us. That we all loved Caprice. Was that true?

I squinted at Angel. His emotions were always shut down when around her. Maybe not shut down, but reined in for sure. What was he hiding?

I cleared my throat. "The last rebellion is too fresh in everyone's memory. It would be the three of us against the Tromara. And we all know how that would end."

"Then I'll take her and run," Jaxon said.

A sharp pang—jealousy—gripped my chest. Jaxon thought he was Caprice's man. But she hadn't decided yet. And maybe she wouldn't choose only one of us, if this whole dragon-shifter and multiple mates information was reliable. He didn't know about her kissing me that second time. And he didn't know how I felt about her.

"Not a chance, man," Angel said. "You'd be putting all our families in danger. Don't get crazy."

Before I thought better of it, I said, "Besides, she's not just yours, Jaxon."

"What the fuck does that mean?" His tone was icy.

I dropped my gaze. "You were there when May told us about dragon-shifters being polyamorous." I steeled myself to look at him. "I didn't risk my life to rescue her for your sake. And I didn't do it because I like Caprice as only a friend either."

The waves of jealousy coming off him made me tense up, ready for a fight. Before, when I thought Caprice would only choose one of us, I'd been willing to accept that she'd go for Jaxon. But now...if she wanted me too, then for once in my life, I wasn't going to step aside. Jaxon couldn't have it all, all the time.

We stared at each other, neither of us willing to back down. When Angel spoke, it took a moment for his words to register: "My wolf has claimed her."

Jaxon and I turned our attention on him.

Angel wore a pained expression. "I thought I could shake it off, you know? Give myself enough time and space, and it would go away. I thought I had it under control. But then that Tromara fucker...what he said he was going to do to her...I lost my shit."

Several heartbeats of silence followed Angel's confession.

"What do you mean by your...wolf...claimed her?" I asked.

Angel rubbed the back of his neck. "Werewolves mate for life once we find our partner. The wolf part of me has decided that my life partner is Caprice."

Jaxon abruptly stood. His hands balled into fists as he glared down at Angel, then he headed for the door.

"It's not like I had a choice," Angel called after Jaxon.

The door slammed shut so hard behind him that the frame rattled. Angel's grief nearly overwhelmed me.

"Damn, I didn't want to let this come between us," he said. "It's not like my father will let me marry her." He hung his head. "What am I going to do now?"

I took it as a rhetorical question. What were any of us going to do now?

24

CAPRICE

My hands wouldn't stop trembling. I trudged across the vacant lawn toward Academy Hall. About an hour after the Tromara left, the summons arrived from Jaxon. I was to meet him in his office immediately.

The fact that he was meeting with me, and not the dean, gave me some hope that everything was going to be okay. The Tromara hadn't taken Jaxon, he hadn't been locked up. So what was our punishment? I assumed it had been decided, since Jaxon wanted to talk with me.

Tentatively, I knocked on his office door. The wooden slab swung open. Without a word, he ushered me in and closed the door. His face was flushed and his hair was a mess. His red-rimmed eyes took me in from head to toe.

Had he been crying? My heart sank. This couldn't be good.

"What is it? What happened?" I asked, reaching for his arm.

His muscles felt as solid as stone under my palm. He didn't react, didn't reach for me. His gaze swept over my face as his brows drew together in a frown.

When he spoke, his voice was flat. "The Tromara have decided on a punishment for our crimes." Jaxon visibly swallowed. "For restitution they demand...you."

"Me? What do you mean? How—?"

"Their king will take you as his wife." He got the words out quickly.

I let my hand drop to my side. Stunned, I didn't know what to say. An image of a large, greasy-haired, dead-eyed man filled my mind. The stench of decaying blood. Being surrounded by violence and fear. A slave for life. It was a worse fate than death. But I deserved it. At least the Tromara hadn't punished the guys.

"I see," I whispered, the vague statement covering for my frenzied emotions and thoughts. A part of me was resigned to my fate, another part wanted to scream, and cry, and run. To rewind my life to before I knew anything about supernaturals. Then came the anger. The rage of helplessness swelled in my gut.

"God damn it!" Jaxon's veneer of composure shattered. He wrapped me in his strong arms, burying his face in my hair. "I don't know what to do—" His voice broke. "For once in my life, I don't know what to do."

I held onto him with equal ferocity, inhaling his oatmeal spice scent. My inner dragon stirred. I wanted to protect him, to make everything okay.

Inspiration struck so suddenly, it sent a physical jolt through me. Instantly, I knew Jaxon would hate the idea.

I spoke against his chest. "I killed those other two Tromara, let me kill their king too." Then we'd all be safe. I could look at the king claiming me as an opportunity rather than a burden. This would get me close enough to him to kill him.

He pulled away only far enough to meet my eyes. "No. You're not going anywhere near him."

I sighed, already exasperated and we hadn't even started to argue yet.

"I'm serious, Caprice. You don't know what you're talking about. The Tromara we fought in the woods were unskilled compared to their king." He cringed. "Angel attacked him at the meeting—"

"What?"

"And he just flicked his wrist, and Angel went down. It was nothing to him. He could kill us all in a heartbeat." Jaxon's hands slid to my waist. "We'll figure something out. We have to. I won't let him take you. Neither will Isabella."

I didn't feel like arguing. My mind was made up about what I was going to do. Where I got the nerve, I had no idea, but suspected it had to do with my inner dragon. I was going to use the rest of this year to learn and prepare. When the time was right, I'd chop the head off the Tromara snake. No one was going to talk me out of this.

My bravado died down. I must be insane to think I could do what no other supernatural had been able to do before. An unnatural warmth spread over my skin, tingling. But those who'd tried weren't dragon-shifters.

"Did you hear me?" Jaxon asked. "You're not—"

I stretched up on my toes, silencing him with a kiss.

Jaxon pulled back. "He also forbade me to touch you. If anyone sees us it will bring more trouble. From now on—" He grunted, bent and kissed me back. "This is our secret. You understand?"

"Yes. I won't tell a soul." In that moment, I realized Jaxon was as much of a trouble-maker as me. We were so alike. Kindred spirits.

He ducked down, angling his head to better ravage my mouth. His tongue slid between my lips, teasing and tasting before plunging inside. I moaned into his open mouth.

Heat pooled between my legs. My fingers laced through his silky hair, pulling him closer, as I pressed my aching breasts against his hard chest. My whole body felt tight and flushed. I needed him. Wanted him more than anything in that moment.

Teacher and all, he was mine.

He eased his tongue out of my mouth to lick my swollen lips. Taking my bottom lip between his, he sucked on it, then nipped at it. His teeth grazed down my jawline, down my neck. He licked the hollow at my collarbone.

My hands slid over Jaxon's powerful chest, down his abs, to his jeans where I found the hard length of his erection. Gently, I ran my fingers over it. His breath hitched. He rocked his hips, rubbing himself against my hand. I undid the button and zipper to free him.

When I wrapped my hand around his hot cock, his eyes closed. He let out a primal groan.

"Oh, Caprice, that feels so good." He groaned again. With his eyes closed and his lips slightly parted, he looked like a golden god in ecstasy. I ran my tongue over those lips as I continued to stroke him, applying a little more pressure.

He growled. "Fuck, girl, you're killing me."

"Take your clothes off," I whispered against his lips.

He slid his jeans and boxers over his narrow hips. I released his cock, so he could finish discarding his pants. He pulled both his button-down shirt and the T-shirt beneath it over his head, adding them to the pile on his office floor. With lust-filled eyes, he stood before me in all his naked glory. There wasn't a shy bone in that man's magnificent body.

For a second, I felt out of my depths. I'd had brief sex with a boy when I was sixteen, mostly as a rebellious act. It had been awkward and uncomfortable. Once I'd declined the offer for a second round, we never spoke to each other again. Shortly after that, I moved to a new foster home.

The man standing in front of me was no boy. Fine golden hair covered his chest and powerful thighs. My pulse raced with a mix of anticipation and nerves. He knew what he was doing. I was just letting instinct guide me, blindly plowing full ahead.

"Are you okay?" Jaxon asked. He must have caught a sense of my trepidation. "We don't have to—"

"No. I want to." My mouth twisted in a wry little smile. "I just... don't have much experience."

His brows lifted. He closed the distance between us. "That's okay."

His fingers caressed my cheek. "It works best if we're both naked," he said with a naughty grin.

I gulped. Even my first time, I hadn't been naked.

"May I?" Jaxon asked, his fingers tugging at the hem of my sweater.

I nodded.

Slowly, he lifted the sweater off over my head. The backs of his hands trailed down my sides, leaving gooseflesh along their path. He undid my jeans, helping me step out of them. Bowing his head, he kissed my cleavage, his fingers making quick work of the bra closure. Once the bra fell away, he palmed my breasts, feeling their weight.

"You're so beautiful." He kissed me long and slow, while teasing my nipples until they hardened. The warmth from his body heated my skin. His erection pressed against my stomach. I felt light-headed.

By the time he released my mouth, I was panting. A dull ache throbbed between my legs.

He took a nipple in his mouth, caressing it with his tongue. I moaned, pressing into his mouth. With one arm around my waist, his free hand slid between our bodies, and into my panties. He slid a finger over my wet core. My knees gave out, but Jaxon held me in place.

"Please," I begged. He was driving me wild with his fingers and mouth.

In one fluid movement, he peeled off my underwear and swept me into his arms. He sat down on the loveseat against the wall. Turning me in his arms, he positioned me so that I straddled him.

Jaxon took a moment to wave a hand over his crotch. Catching my quizzical look, he said, "Protection." I was grateful one of us was thinking straight.

He held my hips, slowly lowering me onto his cock. I gasped as he slid me down his hard length. My inner muscles relaxing to accommodate his girth. All the way in me, he paused, leaving one hand on my hip while the other massaged my breasts.

Then he set a slow rhythm, up and down. Jaxon kissed me slow and sensual. He moved his lips to my nipples. As pressure and heat built in me, I tried to speed up, but he held my hips steady. I whimpered.

"Patience," he said, taking my ravaged nipple in his mouth again.

I threw my head back, digging my fingers into his shoulders. My core tightened, promising release, but he wasn't giving it to me.

He ran his hot tongue up my neck. A smug, masculine grin pulled at his lips. "You want to come?"

"Yes," I breathed.

"Say my name."

"Jaxon."

He gripped my hips with both hands, holding my body in place as he pumped into me. My breath came in quick, shallow bursts as my core tightened.

"Say it again." He groaned, thrusting faster. Those intense grey eyes focused completely on me.

"Jaxon!" I exploded in a mind-shattering orgasm.

His features twisted in sexual agony as a prolonged growl wrenched from his throat.

I collapsed against his heaving chest. His arms surrounded me, clutching me to him. I let myself float, eyes closed, listening to the sound of his heartbeat. The fine, golden hair on his chest tickled my cheek.

"How are you feeling?" he asked, his warm breath on my neck making me shudder.

"Mmmm," I answered.

I could hear the smile in his voice when he said, "That good, huh?"

Jaxon slid me off of him. He settled back, with his long legs hanging over the side of the loveseat, and nestled me next to him. He took the soft, fuzzy blanket that was folded on the back of the couch and spread it over us.

I snuggled into the warmth of him. I could have stayed there forever and been happy.

A while later I was dressed, being nuzzled from behind by a shirtless Jaxon. I'd been trying to leave his office for at least the past twenty minutes. But neither of us could keep our hands off each other.

"I really need to go." I tried for a stern tone, and failed because I couldn't stop smiling.

"What's the rush?" He lips seized my earlobe.

"I'm supposed to be confined to my room, unless I've been directly summoned." I knew it was a lame excuse. The truth was I didn't want to press my luck. Any moment we'd find something to argue about and it would ruin the memory of this time together. I wanted to preserve this in my mind—untainted.

"I did directly summon you," he said into my hair.

Plus, my heart was still fluttering. I had to get some distance, and with it a bit of perspective. I had a feeling I was developing, well, feelings for Jaxon. Like real and intense ones. Or was that just the euphoria from sex?

"Why don't you come upstairs—"

Two knocks sounded on the door. "Jaxon? You in there?" It was Angel.

"Shit!" Jaxon scooped up his shirt, trying to separate the T-shirt from the collared one.

"Dude, I need to talk to you," Angel said through the door.

Jaxon was acting like a teenager caught with a girl in his bedroom by his parents.

"What are you doing?" I asked. "Should I let him in?"

"No!" He raked a hand through his hair. "Fuck. Yes, we'd better deal with this now."

Anxiety flooded my veins at his tone. Did he not trust Angel to keep our secret? "Deal with what?"

"Just let him in." He sounded resigned. But to what?

I opened his office door. Angel's eyes widened at seeing me there, then he glared past me at Jaxon.

"You son of a bitch!" Angel charged into the office. He walked right up to Jaxon and punched him in the face. Then continued to pummel him, calling him all kinds of horrible names.

I clamped my hands over my mouth. What the hell was wrong with Angel? Or, rather, what the hell had Jaxon done to deserve this? He wasn't fighting back, but taking each hit with a grimace.

Liam strode into the room. Immediately, he was pulling Angel off Jaxon. Once he'd managed to separate the two, he placed himself between them.

"What is going on?" Liam asked, bewildered. "What happened?"

Angel's eyes glowed yellow, he growled. "That son of a bitch had sex with her. He thought he could prove that she's all his. Sneaking around behind our backs—even after what we talked about."

Whoa. What the fuck?

Clarity shone in Liam's gaze. His lips tightened in a firm line. "Is this true, Jaxon?" His tone held both disappointment and hurt.

"I didn't plan for this to happen. It just happened. I wasn't trying to be sneaky." Jaxon returned Angel's glare.

Liam turned to me. "You should leave, Caprice."

"I don't think so." I folded my arms. "What's going on?"

"We're fighting over you," Jaxon said.

I took in each of their expressions. He wasn't joking. "That's ridiculous," I said. "Why would you do that?"

"Because we're a bunch of jealous idiots." Liam sighed. "You may have to choose one of us."

My inner dragon lashed out, filling me with annoyance. This was so unfair. They could't tell me what to do. Or who to love. Or even who to lust after.

I studied the three of them. Already, I was developing feelings for Jaxon, maybe ones beyond simple lust. A fluttering tickled in my stomach.

Then there was Liam, sweet and hot. My chest welled with longing for him. He'd avoided my advances before, but wouldn't tell me why. Maybe he'd changed his mind?

Angel was still a mystery. So reserved, yet he made my pulse race. He'd nearly beaten Aimes to death—for me.

I couldn't choose between them. It was impossible. And I shouldn't have to, right? Being with only one man went against every instinct my dragon-shifter had. At the same time, it seemed selfish to have all three of them. If that was even possible. Was it?

I lifted my chin. "No. I'm not going to be some prize for one of you. And I won't choose between you, so...you *all* will just have to figure out how to make this work." Since we were apparently *all* going against the king's orders. This was our secret now. I backed into the hallway, leaving Jaxon, Angel, and Liam in stunned silence.

25

CAPRICE

I walked the outer campus pathway with May. We were both bundled up in thick layers, leaving boot prints in the couple inches of snow that had accumulated so far that night. In a matter of hours the Academy had transformed into a winter wonderland.

We strolled in companionable silence. The question on my mind was...could I go through with my plan to kill the Tromara's leader? Did he want me because I was unique, being a dragon-shifter? How powerful was I compared to other supernaturals? Did anyone know?

He could be afraid of me. Wanting to keep me close so I couldn't pose a threat to him. Too many possibilities swam around in my brain. And a lot of hopeful thinking.

"Now that we know I'm a dragon-shifter," I said, "do you think we can believe the theories in the books?"

May's breath escaped in a foggy cloud. "I don't know. When the Council Queen—Isabella—gets back to you, we'll know more. I hope. In the meantime, Dean Wright has agreed to let you switch over to shifter classes. We'll move you into the shifter dorm, too."

I wondered what was taking Isabella so long. She did have to talk to the European Supernatural Council, then they had to find other dragon-shifters—if there were any. It could be months before they had any news for us. And unless I managed to get out of the Culling Club, I had less than five months before the Tromara took me.

Not losing hope was going to be a real challenge. I knew what I needed to do, but I was alone with my plan to defeat the Tromara from the inside. The guys would shut me down in an instant. May...I didn't want to get her involved. Yep, I was completely on my own.

May eyed me. "Liam told me what happened between you and the guys."

I snorted. "Yeah, that's a mess."

"It will be okay though. I have complete faith that they'll work it out with you."

I wasn't so sure. The last thing I wanted to do was drive a wedge between them. They'd been friends since childhood. Who was I to endanger their friendship? I felt guilty about telling them I wouldn't choose. Maybe I should take it back.

Jaxon was great. I really liked him. But if I chose him, would that really save his friendship with Liam and Angel? Or would it make the whole situation worse?

The bigger question was, could I go against my nature and be only his?

None of this would matter if I was enslaved by the Tromara for life. Learning how I could defeat them needed to be my number one priority.

"You're quiet tonight," May said. "Anything on your mind that I can help with?"

I shook my head. "I don't' think so." I glanced at the tall witch. "You're quieter than usual too."

She grimaced. "I know. But it's nothing you or anyone else can help me with."

"So we're both screwed?" I kept my tone light.

"Pretty much. Come on. I'll show you the Freeman Dorm."

A staff member in the Dean's Hall gave me the key to my new room assignment. May and I trudged through the deepening snow toward Freeman Dorm, where the shifter students lived. My room was on the second floor again, this time at the back of the building.

The first thing I noticed was the single bed. "No roommate?" I asked.

May nodded. "Yeah, um." She sighed. "Honestly, Caprice, no one knows what to do with you. We don't know what a dragon-shifter can do, how powerful you might be, or much else about you."

"So, you're afraid of me?"

"I'm not. But the other students might be. Dean Wright met with the shifter teachers, and they have mixed feelings about you." She gave me a sympathetic smile. "Don't tell them I told you any of this. I just wanted to give you a heads up."

She was saying that the shifters weren't going to welcome me. Even among my own kind, I was an outcast. *Deja fucking vu.*

My first class was Shifter Physiology. I sprinted up to the third floor in Fotia Hall, muttering curses at myself for being late. This Hall had the same layout as Gi and Aeras on the other side of the big lawn. Made from blocks of stone, with thick wooden doors, it held three floors of various types of classrooms.

I stepped into an auditorium style room where the teacher had already begun today's lecture. He was an attractive, massive black-skinned man with short hair, dressed in the instructor's uniform of trousers and white dress shirt. Behind him, on the chalkboard, was a name: Montrell Freeman.

Freeman. As in Freeman Hall, and the shifter family that sat on the Supernatural Council.

I took a seat in the back row. Mr. Freeman halted his lecture, staring at me with intense hazel eyes.

"That's a five point deduction for tardiness, Ms. Sorrentino." His voice was low and silky smooth.

I gaped at him. He was taking points away from me?

Without thinking, I said, "I'm already at the bottom of the points board."

"That's another five points for talking back." Montrell Freeman launched back into his lecture. Which I was too annoyed to pay attention to.

I gritted my teeth. Obviously, this guy wanted me gone sooner than later. The Tromara would either take me at the end of this year, if I was culled, which was looking pretty damned likely right now, or when I graduated next year. I sucked in a deep breath, trying to settle my nerves.

My preference, of course, was to be taken after graduation. I needed to discover, and then master my dragon-shifting skills. I needed to learn how to defeat the king.

I looked hard at the teacher. He avoided my stare, focusing his attention on the front row as he spoke. I might also find time to figure out why Montrell Freeman, fellow royal and heir to the shifter council seat, disliked me so much.

To be continued...

For updates on this series and to get the free prequel novella, join my newsletter at www.CassiaBriar.com

ACADEMY OBSCURA: THE FIERY SHIFTER - CHAPTER ONE

I was sitting in my dorm room doing the first homework assignments for winter term when a knock sounded on my door. I scrambled off the bed and went to answer it. My brows rose in question as I gazed up at Liam's handsome face.

"We want to talk with you about...us," he said, searching my eyes.

I nodded, grabbed my coat and stepped into the hallway. "Do they always send you to get me, or do you volunteer?" It sure seemed like every time the guys wanted to talk to me, Liam appeared at my door.

His moss green eyes sparkled. "I volunteer. I use my fae emotion-sensing advantage as the primary reason that it should be me."

"So you always know how I'm feeling?" That thought unsettled me.

He nodded.

"Doesn't that get exhausting?" I walked with him into the cold night air, not having to ask where we were headed. We always met up at Jaxon's apartment in Academy Hall, which was next door to where I lived with the rest of the beast-shifters and shapeshifters in Freeman Dorm.

Liam chuckled. "Sometimes."

My heart fluttered at the warm sound of his laugh.

"But I couldn't imagine life without it," he continued. "Not sensing emotion for me would be the same as being blind or deaf to you."

I glanced at him as we strolled along the well-lit pathway. His unruly red hair fell across his forehead. Below a faint smattering of freckles across his nose, were the most luscious ruddy lips.

He cleared his throat, most likely getting hit with a wave of my lust. There wasn't anything I could do about the lust, it seemed to go along with being a dragon-shifter. As did wanting more than one man. I hoped Liam, Jaxon, and Angel had worked out a way that I didn't have to choose. I told them I wasn't going to be some prize for one of them. If they wanted me, they'd have to share.

"I'm sorry it's taken me so long to say this," Liam said, "but I wanted to thank you for saving my life in the woods. Those Tromara took me completely off guard. Anyway, thank you."

"You're welcome." An embarrassed blush heated my face. "Though, I still owe you big for how many times you came to my rescue last term." I owed all three of them.

Liam smiled down at me. "You don't owe me. I like being your knight in shining armor whenever I can."

I touched his bicep. "You're sweet."

He cringed.

"What? I'm sorry. I—"

He halted, turning to face me, his hands on my shoulders. He gave them a gentle squeeze. "No man wants to be called sweet."

I had a feeling his reaction was more personal than that. Liam totally fit in the category of *nice guys finished last*. He was sensitive, sweet, and had no idea how attractive he was. The last thing I wanted to do was make him feel unmanly.

"Okay," I said. "Sorry."

"Don't feel bad." He caressed my cheek.

A shiver ran through me at his touch. I turned my head, planting a kiss in his palm. He sucked in a breath, those gentle eyes becoming hooded with desire.

"We'd better keep walking," he said in a hushed voice.

The sexual tension between us was palpable, as we stood gazing at each other. I glanced at his lips, wanting more than anything to kiss them. But this wasn't the right time. The guys and I needed to figure this out before more feelings were hurt.

With a nod, I started walking again, picking up the pace. Liam took a couple of long strides to catch up.

In Academy Hall we climbed the stairs up to Jaxon's apartment. Suddenly, my heart was in my throat, my palms growing moist. What if we couldn't figure this out? What if I caused these guys to have a falling out? They'd been best friends since childhood. I couldn't do that to them.

Liam noticed my sudden panic. His large hand rubbed my back, sending soothing fae magic into me, which helped a little.

"It will be okay. I promise." He opened the door.

Jaxon and Angel sat on the couch that faced the entrance. They stood as we came in, wearing matching expressions of shy hope. Liam led me to the nearer couch, across the coffee table from the guys, and sat down next to me. He shifted away, putting a little more space between us. I chewed on my bottom lip.

The guys retook their seats, everyone sitting in awkward silence for several heartbeats.

Liam began, "We've talked a lot about this over the past couple of days. About you, and our individual feelings toward you, as well as how to keep the friendship between the three of us from falling apart."

I frowned. Maybe I was being unreasonable, selfish. I opened my mouth to speak, but Liam stopped me by placing a hand on my knee.

"You don't need to feel guilty," he said. "We've had some really good talks. Jaxon did a whole bunch of research from May's sources about dragons taking more than one mate. We can make this work."

"How?" I asked, glancing at the three of them.

Jaxon spoke up. "First of all, you're right. Dragons, according to all of the legends, take multiple mates." His brow furrowed. "Though, most dragon-shifters in the tales are male with multiple wives. Seems fair enough to assume it would be the same for female dragons, that they would have more than one husband. Anyway, they seem to form a family unit. And we," Jaxon gestured to Liam, Angel, and himself, "think we can handle that. In a way, we've been as close as family for a long time."

"Closer really," Liam said.

Angel nodded in silent agreement. I was still mildly surprised that Angel was part of this. I wanted him, but I didn't know how much the feeling was mutual. He was such a mystery, never sending any clear signs of how he felt about me. I guessed I'd find out soon enough.

"However," Jaxon continued, "we would like to keep this arrangement between the four of us, and not let anyone else into it."

"And what, exactly, is this *arrangement?*" I asked.

Angel spoke, his muscular arms crossed over his chest. "You'd date the three of us. Only the three of us." The possessiveness in his voice sent a warm pulse through my stomach.

"Okay... What do you have in mind? How would that work?" I asked.

"We thought dividing up our time would be the most fair," Liam said. "Weekdays would be your own. We usually eat dinner together here, you're welcome to join us. Then weekends, we would rotate though. So, this coming weekend is for you and me. Next weekend you'd have Angel to yourself, and the following would be Jaxon. Then the cycle would repeat."

"Wow. You guys have really thought this through. How'd you come up with the schedule?"

Jaxon snorted. "We drew straws, obviously I was the loser."

Oh, my God. Drew straws? That was both sweet and disturbing.

Liam leaned toward me. "So? What do you think?"

I glanced at them all again. "I think it's very unconventional, but fair." I wondered how this worked back when there was a whole dragon society. At that time, among them, this would have been normal.

"You agree to the schedule?" Jaxon asked. "And to only dating us?"

I smiled. "I completely agree. Besides, I don't think I could handle any more testosterone in my life."

Liam gave my knee a squeeze. Jaxon returned my smile, the mirth softening his steely grey eyes. Angel's glowing yellow gaze studied my face and, as usual, I couldn't tell what he was thinking. Hopefully, I'd find out next weekend.

"I should get going," I said, standing. My head was spinning a bit from all this—could it really work? My heart was pounding too fast with anticipation. This was really happening. Then, like a frigid splash of water, reality hit. "What about the Tromara?"

All three men tensed. Our fantasy world of romance could come crashing to an end in five months. Or, it could last a year and five months. Either way, when the Tromara king came for me, I'd be torn away from these guys. I didn't want that to happen, even temporarily. I had to remember my goal: Kill the king.

Jaxon said, "I'm going to talk with Isabella about that. As far as I understand it, under the terms of the Truce, a student may be taken only if they are in the culling. If you can get out of that, then the Council may be able to keep you from the king."

"Since you're also the Council Queen's only heir," Liam said, "they should be able to make a good case for you. King Sebastian was over-stepping when he laid claim to you as his wife anyway."

I frowned, biting my lip. If the king took me then I would take the opportunity to kill him. If he didn't then I wouldn't be forced to attempt the impossible.

"I thought the Tromara had the final say in everything. That they can basically do whatever they want. Is that not true?" I asked.

Jaxon shook his head. "They do and they don't—it's complicated. Just like last summer when they could have taken me for interfering on the full moon, Isabella negotiated an alternative. She has the authority to do the same for you." He ran his fingers through his wavy blond hair. "The Tromara will probably require a sizable sacrifice in exchange for your life. The point is, they want to keep the Truce and the peace as much as we do."

I was horrified at the idea that several more people could die in order to save my life. I shuddered. If I was taken by that monster, I would at least *try* to kill him. I'd rather die than be his slave for life, of that I was sure. But, if there was a chance to appease him in some other way... Could I live with myself for sacrificing others for my life? No.

Part of me wanted to seize the opportunity to end the king's life. That was the original plan I'd come up with when I'd heard he wanted to take me for his wife. Another part of me was terrified of pursuing that idea. I'd had some time to think about it and cool down. I had no training. I barely knew how this world worked. And the king had *magic*. If there was a way out... But at what cost to my soul?

Last term the Tromara had demanded a culling for Jaxon's crime. He'd saved my life last summer, when I didn't know any of this existed. That was his crime. Did the deaths of those students still haunt him?

Liam took my hand, gently squeezing. "We'll know more once Jaxon talks to Isabella. In the meantime, let's try to live our lives."

I glanced down at Liam, who was still sitting on the couch. "You all know I'm not particularly good at following rules, but I don't want to make this worse by openly defying the Tromara." The fucking Tromara didn't own me, but I wanted to keep the guys as safe as possible, and that meant not pissing off the evil bastards' king.

"I agree," Jaxon said. "We need to keep our arrangement to ourselves. Let's be careful with this. No one else needs to know about it."

I cringed, saying, "Maybe we should wait until I'm out of the culling and Isabella has come up with a solution." I hated admitting defeat. I hated giving in to the Tromara.

Angel shook his head. "That's not necessary. The Tromara would have to find out about the four of us. They aren't allowed to stay on campus, and no one here is going to tell them anything. Even Dean Wright doesn't want trouble. She wouldn't turn us in if she found out."

It seemed like a good enough argument. As long as we stayed within the Academy walls, the Tromara wouldn't find out about me and the guys.

"Okay," I said, only half convinced that this was the best thing to do.

"It's a total shit situation," Liam said. "In the mean time, let's make the best of what time is given to us."

"I'd like that." My heart raced, as my brain processed all of this. We were defying the Tromara—but I didn't want to live in fear of them. There was a chance that I'd never be taken away, and that I could have these three gorgeous men for the rest of my life. Hope filled my chest.

Hope was a dangerous thing to hold on to, but right now it was all I had. I slipped my hand from Liam's. "I should go. I'll see you guys later."

They all stood, walking with me to the door. At the threshold I turned, gazing up at each of them. My inner dragon swelled with an unabashed smugness. Mine. A blush crept up my neck. This was going to take some getting used to.

We murmured our goodnights, and I left.

Outside, in the freezing January air, I decided to take care of some business before heading back to my dorm. The past couple of days my new teacher, Montrell Freeman, had been doing his best to keep me in the Culling Club by docking my points.

Entering the Dean's Hall, I stood in the deserted lobby staring up at the magical scoreboard. The numbers glowed next to each student's name, showing their standing at Academy Obscura. Near the bottom, at the ten percent mark, a red line divided those safe from the culling and those who would be sacrificed at the end of the year. Which would be the second round of sacrifices this year. Anger clenched my gut. All of the college age supernaturals were corralled into the Academy and ten percent of them were lined up for the slaughter. This year there were nineteen spots in the culling. It was so unfair.

My name was at the very bottom of the board. I was so screwed. The hope I'd felt with the guys shattered. I was going to become the Tromara king's slave—worse, his wife, which was probably a sex slave. Then I'd live and die at his whim.

Biting the inside of my cheek, I pushed down the hopelessness and tears. If I was going to make it through this, I had to live in the present not the future. The future was too bleak.

I turned and went back through the thick wooden door. My heart heavy.

Although the snow had melted and not returned, icy rain drifted down to melt on my nose. I pulled up the hood of my coat, then headed toward Freeman Dorm.

The hour had gotten really late, and the campus grounds were deserted. On my way to the dorm, I had to pass by Academy Hall again. All the windows were dark. Were the guys asleep already?

A giddy happiness welled in my chest, making me feel like an emotional yo-yo. Tomorrow I'd have dinner with them, then hang out with Liam on the weekend. A yearning swept through me. I'd had crushes before, even on some of my high school teachers, but nothing compared to how I felt about Liam and Jaxon, and to a lesser extent Angel because I didn't know him as well.

I was so glad we'd talked, and had a plan to try. Having to choose between them would have left my heart broken. They were each so different, yet sexy in their own ways. I liked how willful and passionate Jaxon was, even if his affection came through as anger at times. We'd had a rough start, that was for sure. I finally figured out that his distance and general asshole behavior had been to hide his feelings from me, which he'd succeeded in doing until last week.

Now, I didn't know exactly how he felt about me, but I knew he cared. He'd been *crying* for fuck's sake, two days ago when he thought he was going to lose me to the Tromara. My chest clenched at the memory.

Liam was the opposite of Jaxon, always soothing and sweet—except his kisses, they were savage in the best way possible. He didn't hide how much he cared, and I liked that about him.

And Angel...so mysterious. He was a werewolf, deadly and vengeful—he'd proven that several times. Often, I felt that I should be afraid of him, but I wasn't. His primal side attracted my inner dragon like no one else.

Academy Hall paralleled the pathway to Freeman Dorm. On a whim, I decided to avoid some of the icy rain by going through the building instead of walking beside it. Pulling open the door to the massive structure, I slipped into a slightly warmer corridor. At least it was dry. The stone walls held dimmed sconces at even intervals.

The main floor was all offices, shut up tight after hours. Unhurriedly, I shuffled down the hallway toward the opposite door, grinning like a love-sick idiot while thinking about the beast inside Angel and how I wanted to let it out.

My smile faltered as movement down the next hallway caught my eye. I squinted into the dim light. Kneeling by a closed door, was the outline of a familiar red-haired woman. She was muttering, wand in hand.

Quietly, I approached her. "May?" I whispered.

She leaped to her feet, eyes wide, a hand flying to her chest as she turned toward me. "Caprice! My God, you scared me half to death!"

The plaque on the door read: Ms. Duinn. I'd caught May in front of this office door before. This time, I wanted answers.

I eyed her. "What are you doing messing with Ms. Duinn's door?"

May lowered her gaze to the floor. "I can't tell you." Resuming her instructor attitude, she put a hand on my shoulder and pulled me with her down the corridor. "Just forget that you saw me. I don't want you getting into trouble."

"*Me* getting into trouble?" I halted, crossing my arms over my chest. "What's going on? You've been hiding something for months."

She glanced around the empty hall. "Come with me."

A few doors down, May flicked her wand to let us into her office, then switched on a floor lamp by the door. Instead of going to the chair behind her large desk, she took a seat in the little sitting area. I sank into the upholstered chair on the other side of the little round table.

For a long moment, she didn't speak. Her body was so still, I could barely see her breathing. When I was about to press her with more questions, she opened her mouth.

"Look," she said, "I need you to promise that this will stay between us. You can't even tell my brother."

I lifted a brow. This must be serious if she was keeping it from Liam. "I promise."

"I'm only telling you about this because you keep catching me—and we're friends." She visibly swallowed. "And I need to tell someone. I don't know what to do…"

Reaching out, I gently gripped her arm, giving my support.

"For the past two summers…there's been a guy…Josh, that I've been seeing." May stared down at her entwined fingers as she spoke. "We've gotten really serious. Problem is, he's human. My parents would freak if they found out. I-I haven't told him I'm a witch. It's a mess."

"What does this have to do with Ms. Duinn?" I asked.

May grimaced. "She found out about us. Ever since I was her student, she's held a grudge against me. She likes making my life difficult. I thought that would end once I came back as a fellow teacher, but it hasn't. If anything, she's become worse. Last term, she stole a few letters that he'd written me. Now she's holding them over my head. I don't know what she's going to do. I need to get them back." When May finally met my gaze, her eyes shone with unshed tears.

"She's blackmailing you?"

"Sort of. She might, once she decides what she wants from me." May sniffed. "I've been trying to break into her office. That's where the letters are, I think. But her warding charm is too strong."

Wow. That was not at all what I thought was going on in May's personal life. That sucked. Ms. Duinn was a twisted enough person that I had no doubt she'd go through with blackmailing May.

"I'm sorry," I said, not knowing what else to say.

May let out a frustrated grunt. "I'm so mad at myself for letting her take those letters. I never should have brought them here. If my parents find out...I'm not really sure what they'll do, but I think I can handle it. They won't turn me over to the Tromara. What I'm more afraid of is her telling Josh that I'm a witch, and him dumping me. Or worse, he'll not even bother to call, and just walk away. I'll never hear from him again. I can't lose him."

"Couldn't you beat her to it, and tell him yourself?"

She sighed. "I should. I know I should, but I'm terrified to do it. We've been together for a year, and I know he thinks there's something weird going on. He hasn't met my family. I don't want to ruin it all. I never meant for it to turn this serious with a human."

I squeezed her arm again. "He'll be happier hearing it from you. Then Ms. Duinn won't have any power over you."

"I know." Her forehead bunched. "Thanks for talking with me about all this."

"Any time." It was the least I could do for her. She'd been there for me countless times so far this year. I stood. "I should get some sleep. So should you."

May nodded. "I'll try."

Get book two at www.CassiaBriar.com

ABOUT THE AUTHOR

Cassia Briar writes paranormal romance with reverse harems, menages, and couples who find their happily ever after.

She lives in the often misty woods outside of Portland, Oregon with her loving husband and five cats. Cassia's an avid reader with a TBR list she'd have to become immortal to get through. Self-proclaimed Slytherin. Lover of coffee, gargoyle and monster art, and Halloween.

Join the Thorny Haven - Cassia Briar's Reader Group on Facebook.

ALSO BY CASSIA BRIAR

Ignite: An Academy Obscura Prequel Novella

Academy Obscura: The Flame Within

Academy Obscura: The Fiery Shifter

Academy Obscura: The Searing Trials

Academy Obscura: The Scorched Summer

Printed in Great Britain
by Amazon

46819096R00142